# of starfish tides
and other tales

suzanne j. willis

TREPIDATIO
PUBLISHING

ISBN: 978-1-68510-033-9 (sc)
ISBN: 978-1-68510-034-6 (ebook)
Library of Congress Control Number: 2022931587

First printing edition: May 6, 2022
Printed by Trepidatio Publishing in the United States of America.
Cover Design by Mikio Murakami
Edited by Sean Leonard
Proofreading, Cover Layout, and Interior Layout by Scarlett R. Algee

Trepidatio Publishing, an imprint of JournalStone Publishing
3205 Sassafras Trail
Carbondale, Illinois 62901

Trepidatio books may be ordered through booksellers or by contacting:
JournalStone | www.journalstone.com

For Mum and Dad
My first storytellers

contents

introduction

A Letter of Recommendation in this, the Third Year of the Plague

Greetings, dear witches, who have found or been found by this book.

I am come to recommend *Of Starfish Tides and Other Tales* — but if you are reading this, then you hardly need such a ploy. You'll already know, or at least suspect, that Suzanne J. Willis is a chronicler of note, a documenter of the glorious strange, a creator of such wonders and horrors as might make a heart sing or the blood curdle. Sometimes both at once.

She writes of hope and despair, of cruelties great and small. Of how the hunger of hearts might be sated — or worsened. How time and touch might march across a body with much the same effect. She'll give you a quote for the cost of a ride with the ferryman and advise how to have it paid by another.

She'll tell you how thresholds might be born and the breaches between worlds located. She knows the ways of the corpse roads, and the maps to life or death. And how such a map might send you home, set you adrift or free, or damn you utterly. She can disclose the means to turn a traveler from your door so you remain forever unfound. Herein are tales of witches' brews, feathers and truths, the enigmas of rag and bone — all of which are heavier than you might think.

Suzanne shares secrets and magic, but do not fear, sisters, for she never tells all. Recipes lack an ingredient, spells a line of instruction, mention of a compass point is lost. But there's a river of words to drown in, should you so wish.

In her pages roam women with clockwork hearts, men with the Midas touch and veins that run as cold as winter. There are gowns made for the grave that will bear you down into the earth. Marionettes who'll take your lifeblood. Feral children and forgotten palaces. The history of those enchanted scarecrows (whatever were we thinking?). The tale of Mara the Gargoyle who crucified a cardinal — a creature after our own hearts, who can deny? She even — *quel scandale!* — mentions the Autumn Queen, whose true name is never inscribed. Who knows how Her Highness might take *that*?

There is the language of cats and crows, the taste of moonlight, and a compendium of uncommon wisdoms:

How the right name can contain a creature and the wrong one set it ablaze.

How a windfall soul, like a windfall apple, is sour.

How women's tears have made the ocean.

How memory is as slippery as any black cat.

How dragonflies carry the souls of the dead.

Suzanne's recountings are a music writ in scars. They mimic the delicate rhythms of the rain, the power of the storm, the songs of dragons, sleep and seas. And there are the still points where the story still sings even after silence has fallen

Like every good storyteller, she curls a lie on the tongue of each truth, and only a few secrets does she give entirely. How to find heart, home and sanctuary in a book. How to remake yourself and choose to live as you wish. And that we are none of us yet fully written.

This is a little book of sheerest enchantment, and in reading it you'll find yourself humming a tune of purest starlight.

Angela Slatter
Brisbane, Australia
29 December 2021

# of starfish tides

and other tales

# of starfish tides

Under the sliver of witchy moon and the single star adorning its side, he emerged from the ocean.

A woman found him in the early morning on the pebbly beach, his tuxedo still dripping its salty story, his tongue silenced by the pearling light.

He seemed to be of the sea itself, intangible enough to melt into its currents and wash away with the tide. Shivering, he walked back towards the water's edge. The woman, soft voiced and gentle, tried to take his arm and sit him down. He shrank from her touch and stared out at the world, as though seeing it for the first time. The sand dunes, the road rising beyond them, the flock of gulls screeching from the rocks; all were frightening in their newness.

Time had ensnared him: he had no connection to the landscape he saw nor to the woman in front of him, but no memory of his past either. Only the shadowy impressions of things he couldn't quite remember. Had he left his secrets and his voice with the leafy sea dragon to guard in its kelp forest?

All he knew was that he came from the sea. The light and the land of this unfamiliar place caged his speech in his chest and stranded him in the here and now.

* * *

The hospital towered behind the tall iron gates, silent and menacing. The doctors led him from the ambulance through its double doors; inside, the air was steeped in the stench of antiseptic and insanity. He answered their questions with silence, refused to even give them his name. In doing so, he denied them a set of words by which to define him, to give him a past and a future. This man of salt and sand remained a mystery.

So they put him in a bare white room and observed him, then in the grounds under the trees shedding their autumn leaves. There were group therapy sessions and alternations between fully medicated and unmedicated. But he remained the same frightened, ethereal creature that had been brought to them from the seashore.

He was harmless, they decided, although his obstinacy frustrated them. Still, what can be done with someone who has no past and won't allow anyone to give them a future? So he wandered the halls and passed vault-like rooms, slipping through the days like silver light on the waves...

...until the day he turned right instead of left, into a room with bars across its arched windows and an old upright piano against the far wall. A memory uncurled deep within him and he sat before the instrument, touching its yellowed keys as tentatively as someone might touch an injured bird.

A note, then two, until his fingers found their rhythm, beckoning forgotten sounds that snaked through the hallways and slunk between barred windows.

The keys sang under his hands, the music calling up his memories from the deep. Notes sprang across the currents, which danced moodily in their wake. A man and his piano were perched on the ocean floor, playing the sea from its slumber. A solitary manta ray gliding wing-perfect above trailed the millennial story of evolution behind it. Sunlight refracted through the water, setting the coral aflame and darting off the tails of the mermaids who had brought the sirens with them to drink in his music.

The ocean heeded his call: the night-feeders and coral polyps were called to life by the symphony, the seahorses and silvery fish balletic in their response. On and on he played, until it was unclear whether the flashing of fins and the mermaids' dance were choreographed to the music, or if the notes were the harlequins of the sea-creatures' whims.

He played through dusk, when the sea turned from golden to emerald then dark. He played through the moonlit hours when the stars peered through the depths and orchestrated their long-ago light around his indigo notes.

Tentacles of the jellyfish hordes, some ropy pink, others whippily thin, mirrored the sirens' hair streaming in the sea's ebbs and flows.

The ghosts of dead sailors from the skeletal wreck, just beyond, watched and listened with phantom hearts that felt love for a moment once again.

He played the sea from its torpor. The music told his story, flitting between his past and the confusion-ridden now.

It may have been a minute, or perhaps a thousand years, when the tune began to fade from his fingers. The music slowed and the ocean drained away, taking the moonlight and starfish with it. His hands stilled; the piano crumbled and twisted into a gnarled old piece of driftwood, worn smooth by countless tides. He thought he heard the mermaids giggle and sigh as they tempted lost sailors to watery graves. Then there was nothing. Only the silence of the rising sun; red, heraldic, beautiful.

And so it was that he had found himself on the pebbly beach, dripping wet and shivering in a tuxedo made for his stage.

* * *

"Hey, Piano Man!"

"Play us a song, Piano Man!" the other patients yelled after him as he wandered through the hospital, out into the manicured gardens on a bright-blue autumn day.

The nurses tried to shush the patients, unwilling to admit that they, too, had felt the strange effects of the songs he played on the old piano. It made them think of waves crashing on the shore and of grey-green stormy skies. It made them feel like something ancient was waiting for them a long way away. They wouldn't speak of it, even with one another, for it unsettled them. But with each day that went by, his breathing had seemed shallower and his skin drier, almost desiccated, like a starfish left in the sun at low tide. They knew that soon the songs would be silenced forever.

A breeze blew across the lawn, shaking loose the leaves. He lifted his head and breathed deeply. There was salt on that breeze, along with the sharp tang of seaweed drying in the sun. He smiled, then, at the familiar taste and smell of the air, knowing that *someone* had heard his call. For under his symphony of sadness and light, he had strung a plea in the only language that he knew; hoping that the notes would find the ones who knew him, even though he no longer knew himself. Hoping the song would call to the ones who could lead him home.

On the back of the salt breeze, a weathered old couple moved through the hospital halls with the sense of wanderers about them, like ancient sea-relics shaped by time. She, a bold ship's figurehead in sea-green, cutting through the air like a prow through water: voluptuous, untouchable. He, with the clackety-clack of hob-nailed boots on a wooden pier, looking like not much more than kelp and rags stretched over old pirate bones. They walked across the lawns, under swirling leaves that moved as though pulled by unseen currents, and smiled as they lifted their silent son to his feet.

The nurses and the patients – it was their turn to be silent now – watched as the three of them disappeared out the gates. All that was left behind was the slightest tang of ocean air, then a sigh of breeze bearing away the last of him to parts unknown.

The couple led him back to the pebbled beach and watched as the sea's touch unfurrowed his brow, as her undulating waves whispered *welcome home*.

He had washed in on a starfish tide, and would return on the eve of the blue moon. The three walked toward their waiting ship, of wooden hull and drowned sailors' dreams, where his past flooded back through him: Neptune's musician sat on his throne of waves and diamond light, as befits the Sea King's favourite courtier.

The woman waded to the bow and fitted herself to the spine of the ship, an ancient figurehead, sanguine in sunset light. The pirate captain, withered and gnarled, took the heavy wheel with the clackety-clack of sea-faring bones. The ship creaked and crashed forward, catching the wind and the breath of the moon behind her.

All conspired to move him onward, to follow his north, to sink beneath the briny, grateful depths and bear home the keeper of the ocean's song.

a silver thread between worlds

**Thomasina – a woman with an empty space where her heart
should be**

"Speak to her," the voice said.

"To who?" I asked. There was no one else in the room.

"You know who."

*I had made it here through a doorway unknown. What was one more
step into empty air? I took a deep breath and began, hoping that it would be
enough...*

Anyone who believes that faeries are wee, golden-haired creatures
with dragonfly wings and sweet intentions has never met a real faerie.
Never crossed the borders, or pushed through the back of the cupboard,
or crawled through a strange, crooked doorway in the base of an old tree,
into the realm where the fae live. If they had, they would know what real
faeries are; the hags and the dragon tamers, the goblin-children and wind
riders. The Heart Keeper.

Of course, you don't have to cross anywhere to find the Heart
Keeper. She and her ilk are still criss-crossing from their lands into ours.
Human hearts are far too tempting for them to stay put and wait for the
brave, the silly, the lucky, and the believers to seek them out. Oh, not the
organ of muscle and ventricles and electric impulses that keep our fragile
bodies going. No, it's much more gruesome than that. Their taste runs to
real hearts, where we keep our desires and fears and love. Strange things
they are, too, and each one a different shape and size depending upon its
owner.

Small and gentle as seahorses, hiding in a kelp forest of shyness;
cumbersome sailor's chests full of scrimshaw love notes in language

unfamiliar; ordinary teacups holding witches' brews of forgotten dreams and hope.

Whatever their measure, they all beat in the same manner. Like burning wood, alight from within, red and white heat moving through them in shifting light. Sparks find their way out, here and there; flames shoot out from the scars of old wounds, licking at the cold air.

These were things that I knew, knowledge that had reached for me across the borders, long before I found myself facing the hearth of the Heart Keeper, looking for my own heart that she had stolen from me years earlier.

* * *

Venya – a wildwood faerie. The Heart Keeper.

Human hearts belong in Faerieland. We Keepers don't have mothers or fathers. So there is no one to teach us this, but we are born with those words on our tongues. They are the very first words that we speak. For the first century or two, I believed it. But I made enough mistakes in that time – do you know how difficult it is for a faerie to admit she has made mistakes? – to know that not all of them should come this way. It's the people who can live quite happily without their hearts that are the best and worst to steal from. The ones who don't even recognise its absence. We *need* them, but too many will irrevocably breach our worlds.

All hearts call for their owner. That's part of the pleasure of taking them. A thin sliver of longing connects the two parts that make a person whole. Some hearts sing softly as evening falls, while others whisper storm words at the height of summer. Others still send snowflakes or raindrops that wisp across the skin. But those whose owners have forgotten them entirely sit silent and cry quietly from time to time. They are the ones that I have learned to use for the most secret of faerie things. From them are born the doorways between Faerieland and the ordinary world.

* * *

Thomasina

I can tell you the exact day when I first realised that my heart was gone. It was hot, the middle of summer, and the wind swirled off the ocean in briny updrafts. A flock of northern kites circled high above, watching the ground. I began to walk and it was only when I had gone the full three blocks toward the beach that I realised they were watching *me*. Had followed me the whole time, calling to me.

I knew, without a shadow of a doubt, that my heart sent them there, to tell me it was waiting for me. For the first time, I keenly felt my loss. The kites called above me, a hollow song that sounded like the end of the world. I bumped down onto the ground, watching them and remembering the long ago night it had been stolen from me. Until that moment, I had always thought that the memory was just the fanciful imaginings of an eight-year-old child.

I had woken suddenly, in the still darkness of the small hours that I now know can stretch on forever. The rocking chair in the corner of my room was gently rocking back and forth. At first, there was just a faint outline of *someone* sitting there. The chair moved back and forth, hypnotic. As I drifted in and out of sleep she came into view, flickering like an old movie, silvery and indistinct. Her hair moved about, as though snaking in the wind. Or was it the gentle writhing of snakes? I smelled earth after the rain; smelled the thunder and storms of Faerieland, although I couldn't tell you how I knew that. That untamed creature sat and rocked in my chair. Then she smiled at me.

In that smile was an invitation. She stretched out her hand.

Come with me, she said.

Even in dreams, that is a scary prospect. I shook my head and her smile faded as I fell asleep again. The next morning, my mother told me I looked pale, and I felt *odd*, although I couldn't quite say why.

I never slept through the night again.

And if the kites hadn't found me that day, years after that strangest of nights, circling overhead and calling out sadness, I might never have known why.

* * *

Venya

Human hearts taste like faerie food. Although part of being the Keeper is to stop those precious kernels from falling into the hands of other faeries. I haven't always been successful, but that wasn't *always* a mistake. Long ago – longer than three of your lifetimes – the Autumn Queen decreed that at the solstice feast, the heart of a babe was to be joined with lightning from the Dark Music mines. That dish was hers alone to consume. Afterwards, she danced the rowan-tree waltz. It was marvellous to see her, moving like a tree bends in the tempest, like the willow sings to the waters flowing under it. The waltz meant that for the next year, no rowan tree branches could be used by people to escape dancing in a faerie ring. Although why they would want to escape, I don't know.

Then came the year when, instead of a babe's heart, that of a dying miser was used instead. There was something just as magnificent in watching the Queen try to dance within the enormous circle of *amanita muscaria* mushrooms as she grew thick roots into the earth and sprouted red berries from her slender branches that spread outwards.

In the stillness afterward, we could still hear the beetle-tick of her pulse.

It might seem strange to you for Faerieland to have a rowan tree as Queen for the next hundred years or so, but she did quite nicely, thank you. And I couldn't keep giving over baby's hearts forever. What kind of keeper would I be? We all need to find our own way and sometimes – the best times – that way is roundabout and not at all straight.

So, keep them we must, and not be frivolous in the taking or the giving. But it's *using* them that is all-important. That's what keeps them alive, what keeps that thin silver thread between the heart and its owner from breaking. It's when we add not-so-human things – a little drop of poison, a wishbone with a forgotten wish clinging inside – that they tug on that thread.

* * *

Thomasina

I wish that a missing heart just left behind an empty space, a neatly cauterised wound that no one could ever see. But that space is filled up all too quickly with things hungrily looking for a home. And those things have voices that whisper constantly, reminding me that I will never be enough. Will never fit in, no matter quite where I go.

It was only when I realised what it was that was gone that I began to *revel* in my differences, in not fitting in. There was freedom in it. I sang down the silver thread, no matter where I was – walking along the streets, standing in a packed train – without a care for the strange looks I got. I pushed against the backs of cupboards and looked for strange creatures that might be hopping, ready to give chase. Although I had no words for it, I began to believe that there was another world, just an edge away from my own, and that if I turned the right corner or the right key, I would find it. The frost-mouth faeries breathing winter, the silver spinners weaving wishes into tiny flitting finches, the land that is forever autumn, gold and whispering and spider web fine.

* * *

Thomasina's Heart

Find an oak tree, one that hides birds' nests in its forks and knotholes. Wait until one of those tiny birds swoops in and lands in its branches. Walk around the tree widdershins, keeping your left hand on her trunk. Thrice will do it. See the bird as she takes off again, the bright blue of her wings flashing in the sun, the touch of white at her throat a patch of spilled moonlight? Those colours are for you. She's carrying your pain with her, will fly up, up, then drop it from on high so it splits into nothing more than dust and star-parts. It will not find you again.

Now you are free to remember the water witch in green's cruel gloom, her smile a saw of pointed teeth. To remember running from her, then carving your name into a frozen pond and watching the nixies, blue and scaled with cold, swim up from the deep and lick the ice clean from underneath, so the letters shone like diamonds. Leaving them there like a dare, for the water witch to find.

She gave your name to the Heart Keeper before you were even born. We have been waiting for you ever since.

* * *

Venya

Not many people understand the language of hearts. Some can't hear it, even when they arrive here. They don't last very long. I often wonder why their hearts call to us faeries in the first place. These aren't the people who have forgotten their hearts. No, they are as ruthless as the goblins that raid the Revenant Lands, taming wraiths to search for graveyard treasures and word souls. They are the ones who never cared that they had ever had hopes or dreams or wishes at all.

A few of those hearts have found their way to the new Queen.

But as soon as I saw Thomasina, I knew she understood. That she could find the door through, because she would hear the calling of forgotten hearts in their guise of secret doorways. That night, as I watched her sleeping through the window, I saw her singing to her own heart in her sleep. I had never seen one like it: a shapeshifter, light and merry and *strong*. One moment a dog gleefully snapping at the sparks its wagging tail sends into the darkness. The next, a mermaid swimming through the invisible currents of night air. Next still, a tiny child in the image of its owner, curled on her chest and mouthing along the words of sleep song.

I was careful as I leant over the sleeping child, held my hand over her chest to find just the right place to cut. My knife was a blade of albatross bone, its handle the scaled skin of a salamander. Together, they were an instrument of fire and ferocity. Only under a faerie hand could it have been wielded as delicately as required.

Pressing the blade down near Thomasina's collarbone, I came within a cat's whisker of her flesh. If the skin is so much as scratched, let alone if blood is drawn, then the prize is lost forever. Collarbone to sternum, then back again, a perfect V-shape. The caul was silky and separated easily, almost as though it wanted to. Then my quarry, in the shape of a northern kite, slipped through. It hovered before me, burning brighter than any earthly flame. With a snip, snap, I opened the cage that sits in the middle of my own chest. It flew in and, as I snibbed the door behind it, I felt it put its head under its wing and fall fast asleep.

And if Thomasina had come with me that night, as she was meant to, she would not have spent years searching and wondering and waiting for the right door.

* * *

Thomasina

I stood atop the mountainside at sunset, barefoot on the ancient, lichen-covered rocks. The breeze blew through the treetops, giving voice to the silvery eucalypt leaves. I don't understand the songs of trees, but you don't need to understand something to know its beauty. That cold evening, I felt like they were singing for me.

Their voices grew louder as the wind rushed up the gully. I stretched out my arms and it pulled them upwards; for a moment, my feet lifted from the earth and I thought I might fly away with it. But the fae do not give gifts so easily. *Especially the wind riders,* I thought.

I had been readying myself for years for this, reading everything that I could to tell how to get to Faerieland. Everything that I loved – stories of magic, faerie tales, blues music sung in a cigarette-and-whiskey voice at 3am, the way the light plays in the air at the moment between dusk and twilight – told me that something else was waiting, just beyond the shadows. After the kites, I had begun to recognise those who still had their hearts and those who didn't. We're an odd bunch, the missing ones. We *knew*, and it was the most delicious secret between us.

Some swam out in dark waters on the new moon, let the waves crash over them, waited for the mermaids to shine a light on the way from their soul-lamps made of sailors' bones and Neptune's glorious hair. Others tried to dance their way there, or walked across the oldest of countries hoping to find a doorway in a mountain, or the Erl-King stepping from an alder tree. On the rare occasion one of them disappeared, we would celebrate with mead and mulled wine. I tried to keep the jealous longing at bay, but sometimes it soured that mead in my throat.

It was only by accident that I found myself on that mountainside, having driven out there to return, of all things, a lost cat that wound up on my doorstep. When I left the owner's house, I saw the kites again, soaring and dipping in a dance that no normal updrafts could create.

Standing on the edge of the mountain, facing the gusting wind that made the leaves sing and soil shake, a warm current slithered toward me. It reached out, wrapped around me, stopped my shivering. I smelled honey and pomegranates. Then, for only the second time in my life, I smelled the thunder of the storms of Faerieland. That otherworld breeze had a forgotten heart's voice.

Jump, it whispered. *I will catch you.*

As the sun slid down beneath the horizon like a pat of butter, and the clouds flamed crimson and violet and faerie-thunderous, I stepped off the edge of the mountain.

* * *

Venya

You found your doorway. And here you are.

* * *

Thomasina

"Here I am," I nodded.

I had been blown, quite literally, into the home of the Heart Keeper. It was underground, tree roots from which she had hung lamps and dried herbs wending through the room and through the floor. It was lined with shelves, upon which sat delicate glass jars, labelled with sepia ink in a spidery hand. Within each jar beat a heart and they whispered in crystal-plink voices.

Speak to her, my own had said.

"To who?" I asked. There was no one else in the room.

You know who.

So I had told my story, and she had told hers. As if sculpted from her words, the Keeper came into view, shadowy and flickering, then finally taking her full shape as our tales converged with my arrival here.

She stood before me, whole and beautiful, reaching out her hand towards me.

"I've waited a long time," said Venya, standing by the mantelpiece over which hung a bright mirror. "But I know you have searched for much longer. You know how time works between Faerieland and your old world?"

I nodded again. Time is slippery enough in one place, let alone trying to measure it against another one entirely.

"And now you're here, what is it that you will do?"

I looked around, shrugged. I hadn't thought that far ahead. The whispering grew louder. In the mirror, a weathered man in a pork-pie hat leaned against an old fence and played a battered guitar, a cigarette hanging from his mouth. He looked out at me, smiled and lifted his head as though to say, *There you are.*

"Look harder," she said. "You might find it easier if you shut your eyes."

It should have been an odd thing to say, but of course it wasn't. I closed my eyes and, in the darkness, a tracery of light appeared. It was a pair of hands...my hands! I was crouched beside someone sleeping, carefully carving the air above their chest. Then I was holding a jar, dropping in tiny white starflowers to join the spinning wheel heart sitting inside it. My own sat on my shoulder, singing a song of falling in love and the voice she once gave to a man in a pork-pie hat as his fingers flew over the keys of a rickety piano.

I smiled. "What about you?" I asked Venya.

"There is much more to this than 'you' or 'me,'" she smiled. "Are you ready?"

"A lifetime beyond ready," I replied.

She held out her hand to me, and we stood before the mirror together. The old musician looked back at us, tipped his hat. I had never met him, but I knew his voice sounded like gravel and honey, that his songs were vaudeville stories told under witchy moons. On the Keeper's mantel sat his heart, the size of a salt shaker, shaped like a gramophone.

"He's like you," Venya said. "He carries other worlds in the space left behind. He's waiting for you…"

He turned, slung the guitar over his back, and walked toward the dark forest behind him. My reflection and Venya's came into view, sharpened against that silhouetted forest. It was like looking into a dark pool, firelight slipping over its surface. A stone dropped into the pool, rippling its surface, and the reflections wavered. When it stilled again, there was just one. Me, with wild hair and faerie eyes, but something of the human in the chin and ears, the freckles across my skin. I couldn't imagine why I had ever thought that there were two of us there.

In the mirror's distance, the bluesman stopped, turned, beckoned to me. I was ready for him to show me the new doorways we had created with those precious, forgotten hearts. We Heart Keepers don't have mothers or fathers, but we know that human hearts belong in Faerieland. We are born with those words on our tongues and, although I didn't quite know why, I said them aloud as I walked through the mirror.

rag and bone heart

Before my sister, Bess, disappeared, before I met the king, we lived in the shadow of the Stonemen. Life will always be *before* and *after* them; they made us what we were, shaped our lives as though carving them out of the rocks from which they rose.

Bess had been born with the old magic inside her, able to call up the wind and rain from years gone by, or turn unwanted travellers from our door. It marked her as one who would be apprenticed to the rag-and-bone woman, but that was *before* the Stonemen. When Bess turned fifteen, our parents told her that they would come to take her the next day. We knew the step of the Stonemen all too well – a rhythmic, gravelly scrape of footfalls grinding the earth whether path or road or loamy soil. Still, there was something light about them; more like the creep of a child than the heavy step of men. They selected very particular futures for the girls from poorer families, scarring their faces with terrible, thin razors to show the world what the girls were. Three vertical scars on each cheek for a servant; whorls over the forehead, nose, and chin for dancers in the public houses; a single rose on the left cheek with vines trailing down to the chest for the comfort girls who would go with the soldiers to the Cyclene Wars.

In the early hours, when our already-grieving parents had fallen asleep, Bess whispered to me that *no one* was going to carve roses into her skin and that no one was going to do it to her sister either. I was only eight then, and didn't understand what was behind the vacant stares or hoarse whispers of the comfort girls. The ones that returned, anyway.

With a soft snick, Bess opened the door and carried me away from that future. I lay my head on her shoulder, her dress scratchy against my cheek, watching our house get smaller. She sung to me, in her low, sweet voice, sung me into a sleep she wove just for me.

We belong to each other, she said over the years in which it was just the two of us. Then, the day I turned sixteen, the Cyclene Wars ended. The king's heralds sang out victory as we walked the streets freely, watching as the Stonemen fell. Most ground to a halt where they stood; they scattered the shore and huddled, cairn-like, in our town square and on the roadside. Families we knew and ones that we didn't spat on them and carved the names of damaged or long-gone daughters into their hard skins.

Not even the bitter winter that piled snow drifts on the windowsill and froze late bluebirds migrating south in mid-flight could temper our joy. And in the midst of that joy, Bess met her lover.

"We're going to be married, Danae. Then there will be no more of this" – she gestured around our unlit hut, the wind whistling through the wooden boards – "and you can finish your schooling, I promise."

Spring came, though the ground remained frozen and food scarce, and Bess went out one day to the town, a secret smile on her face. Hours became days became weeks; the snow melted and the days grew bright, and still she didn't come home. I should have asked her about that smile, demanded to know the name of her lover.

I scoured the town, but the winding streets and the dark alleyways yielded no sign of her; nor did the woods to the south, or the rough port that lined the shore. After nine torturous days, during which I had no sleep, I returned home exhausted and wretched. I began to drift into sleep just as the sun was setting. A voice through the window jolted me awake.

Danae, sweet girl, it's time to run
through fallow fields, under noonday sun
The old ones wait 'neath the darkening leaves
under inking skies, under broken eaves…

I sat up, strained to hear as the words floated away down the street. It was the dream-casting song she used to sing to me as a child. Bess! I flung open the door and ran down the cobbled, winding streets after her.

They seek to keep you safe and warm
to carve your wings, to sculpt your form…

The gas-lighters lit their lamps and voices spilled merrily from taverns, but I ran only after Bess. There! I ran faster, following her voice as it trilled over the evening sounds of the town and the crying of babes from their cribs within safe, whitewashed walls.

The old ones wait, they are shriven, anew
the old ones wait in the dark, for you…

I skidded around the corner on unsteady legs. The street was empty, puddled with yellow lamplight. Straining my ears, I listened for Bess' song as the evening breeze lifted my hair and cats yowled in the distance.

I had lost her again. Or had she even been there at all?

My knees folded under my weight and I fell, hands scraping against the cobbles. On the cold ground, in the gathering dark, I curled myself into a ball and cried until my throat was raw.

After a long time, there was a murmur of voices and hands lifting me up. They felt as hard and cold as the cobbles beneath me. Then the world went black.

* * *

I woke to new-day sounds filtering through the window above me. The room around me was unfamiliar, with its dark wooden shelves full of glass bottles, mortar and pestles, feathers and bleached animal skulls. Thoughts of Bess ran me through.

"Well, you're awake then," croaked a voice from the other side of the room. A hunched figure in a dirty brown robe was searching through some of the bottles with gnarled, withered hands, his back to me. "We wondered how long you would be out."

He motioned out of the open window to someone, then turned his crinkled-apple face toward me.

"Who's 'we'?" I rose from the bed. "Who brought me here?"

"None less than the king himself, and a few of his men. I am the king's personal apothecary, you know. It's a rare few that he trusts…"

I barely listened as he rattled on. Why would the *king himself* bother with me? I'd heard the stories, of course – everyone had – of how he would take to wandering the towns on certain nights, disguised as a commoner. Some say he had a way of melting into the shadows, of becoming almost invisible, in order to watch his subjects. Some said he was not an ordinary king.

The apothecary ushered me out the door and nodded to the palace guard who was waiting there.

"One more thing, dear. I've been asked to give you this." He held out a small, cream parchment, the king's seal pressed into the shimmering golden wax, then snatched it back as I reached for it. "Of course, I'd be happy to read it for you, if that's not one of your...skills."

"Matter of fact, it is." I was sure that he was wondering, just as I was, what the king could possibly want with me.

* * *

Under the seal of that innocuous parchment was an invitation to walk with the king in his private gardens. I trailed behind the guard as the palace loomed closer, hewn from limestone cliffs. Its pylons and arched windows, intricate carvings and domed roofs stood sentry over the sprawling grounds and the city beyond. Something about it, though – the cold stone, the vastness, the *uncommonness* of it – made me think of a prison.

Inside, another guard with his golden-tipped sword and beaten silver helmet led me through corridors lit with lamps of amethyst and citrine, through great halls with carved amber walls, the ceilings disappearing into the darkness above. The woven carpets beneath our feet soaked up the sounds of our footsteps, as though no one was passing through at all.

He stopped before a door that was ajar and motioned for me to walk through. I found myself outside, on the edge of manicured lawns that rolled and stretched down to a vast lake. Next to a cherry blossom full in bloom stood the king. His arms were bare and, in the sunlight, his skin gleamed as though it was oiled. Dressed in black, he wore no jewellery, not even the monarch's signet.

I curtsied, as I'd been instructed to do, and cast my eyes downward.

"If you look at the ground the entire time, you'll miss the best of my gardens." It sounded like he smiled as he spoke. I looked up and smiled back, although I still felt nervous. He certainly *looked* like an ordinary man and perhaps an ordinary king – but as he was the first I had ever met, how could I really know?

"I have many beautiful things in my gardens and my palace, Danae" – he motioned to me to come forward and we began to walk – "but I daresay that today you are the most beautiful among them."

My dress was threadbare and I knew that sorrow lined my face. "You're very kind, sir."

"How is it that your face was not carved into, like those of the other peasants?"

"I was lucky enough to have someone to look after me," I replied, swallowing my tears.

"The Stonemen did those terrible things without my order or approval. I never condoned such things happening to my own people."

I thought about that time. The Stonemen had worked with his armies and policed the towns. But surely, if the king *had* known their true nature, he would have fallen along with those creatures.

We walked a while in silence, down a winding path lined with blushing purple magnolias and apple trees scattered with tiny, unripe fruit. I gasped and my king laughed softly. In the branches of the trees hung golden cages, with golden statues of finches and nightingales inside them. Shiny-bright peacocks, jewelled with emeralds and sapphires, stood silent on the ground. A hawk, frozen with wings outstretched as though soaring through the skies, shone like a tiny sun from the top of old, gnarled branches.

"So much gold!" The words were out before I knew it. "I'm sorry, I just meant that – I've never—"

He didn't seem to notice. "Tell me – are these not the most beautiful birds you have ever seen?"

As he looked around at his statues, his face was almost reverent; a spot of sunlight refracted off one of them and lit the curve of his throat. An unknown feeling uncurled itself in my stomach, a curious urge: if he had been only an ordinary man, I could have leaned over and kissed that bright spot of vulnerable flesh.

"They are very lovely indeed," I said, knowing that they were far from the most beautiful, having heard magpies calling out through a foggy autumn morning and seen bower birds rummaging through the forest undergrowth for bright blue treasures. But I knew enough not to let him know that we didn't share the same thoughts on beauty.

We walked on, talking about inconsequential things. All around us the golden statues of women scattered through the gardens – sitting on benches, reclining on the perfectly clipped grass, peeking out from behind trees. I blushed when I saw that some of them were naked. The king looked at me then, a strange look of longing that I couldn't quite place. The memory of the whisperings that I had heard about the king, which I had pushed to the back of my mind, wormed their way forward. I realised that what I had felt earlier wasn't desire, but the fluttering of anxiety. My heart beat faster and I fought the urge to flee.

"What troubles you?" he asked. "Is it your sister?"

"How do you know about Bess?"

"You were distraught about her when we found you. And I like to know as much as possible about those who are invited to my palace."

"She would never leave me, never. I can't help thinking something dreadful has happened to her, but I can't stop looking until I find her. It makes me feel like I'm—" I stopped myself. If I *was* going mad, it wouldn't do to tell anyone about it.

"It is a terrible thing, not knowing, and to have to suffer that alone," he said, motioning for me to walk again. We began to circle the lake, its dark waters ruffled by the afternoon breeze. In the shallows I could see glints of gold and wondered briefly how rich he must be to let it lie like that in the muddy water.

"I would very much like to help you, Danae."

"Why?"

"I cannot stand to see a beautiful young woman with a broken heart. I would like to help you find Bess and be the one to mend it for you."

He leant forward and for a moment I thought he was going to kiss me. I froze, but he simply held my hand lightly in his and brushed the back of it with his lips.

As we walked back in the gathering dark, something looked up at me with shiny eyes from the water and I almost cried out. The gold I had seen earlier was, in fact, half-buried statues of women, with jewels for eyes— one with dark quartz, another emeralds, another still with sapphires. Bess once told me that I had eyes like sapphires, but that thought now made me shudder, for those statues made me think of drowned women; ladies of the lake. It was shocking, but when my king looked at me, I forced a smile. The fleeting attraction I had felt earlier disappeared, yet I knew he was the only chance I had to get back Bess.

* * *

It was dark when I got home and I busied myself lighting the lamps, to distract myself from the strange afternoon and the uneasiness it had left me with. In the soft light, I saw that my hand shimmered with a fine gold dust. It made me think of the garden of stillness and shadows, and a king's fancies.

The next day, I went to see the rag-and-bone woman. I thought I could trust her, for the magic Bess and she shared made them almost kin. I hoped she remembered that, for I had only seen her one other time, when Bess and I had been sent by our mother to the port to buy fish. Unburdened by our everyday worries, I had darted through the crowd, Bess laughing after me.

I had run toward the end of the wharf, where the smallest boats were tied and a little knot of people peered down into the water. Curious, I pushed my way through and looked down, wishing I hadn't the moment I saw the body, with its scarred face and mutilated torso, bumping hollowly against the pylons.

Bess had pulled me away and hugged me to her, staring down at the *thing* that was once a girl like me. A woman swaddled in rags and mangy furs had put her hand on my sister's shoulder. It was her – the rag-and-bone woman. She hissed at the crowd to hush, then wiped my sister's tears with a grubby hand, whispering to her before disappearing into the crowd.

Now I needed the rag-and-bone woman's knowledge. It was rumoured that her hand was in the Stonemen's fall, and that she could find unlucky men the lovely wives they hankered after. It was also rumoured that the cost of her services was not cheap. But nothing worthwhile is.

* * *

I sat with the rag-and-bone woman in her hut that smelled of marrow and drying skins. She stared at me across the smoky fire, her eyes obsidian-black and snaky. Only she could tell me how to truly win the heart of the king.

She told me the cost of her spell, cackling through the smoke and the dark. I nodded without hesitation. It seemed a small price to pay, all things considered.

Skin soot-stained by her herb fire, she mixed the spell and chanted over the bubbling pot. Her words made me shiver and sent dark thoughts racing through my head. She put her thumb into the ashes, motioned for me to hold out my tongue, then pressed her thumb onto it. It was like a brand, but I stifled my scream.

Scooping a ladleful of spell-liquid from the pot, she made a sign in the air over it with her hands and held it to my lips. The draught tasted of sage and coated my mouth like candle wax.

"How will I know when to use it?" I asked.

She glared at me, her glittering eyes narrowed. "When he comes to you at dusk and all you have left to give are your words and your kiss, it will be time."

I thanked her as I rose and left the cloying darkness of the hut, wondering if it would be enough.

* * *

The day after that, he sent for me again.

* * *

He had me wait for him in a chamber on the third floor of the palace. Compared to the sumptuousness of rest of it – or the parts that I had seen – the room was almost monastic. Bare stone walls, plain wooden table, a shelf holding violet glass bottles filled with oil, and ancient canopic jars in the corner. The jars were topped with marble lids, carved in the shapes of women's faces – one with eyes of quartz, another with eyes of emerald, the last with eyes of sapphire.

As I heard the king's footsteps on the stairs, then walking softly down the hall, I felt like a child again: ignorant of the world's terrible secrets, but knowing, innately, that they waited to consume me.

With a boldness I didn't feel, I turned to face the door and looked into my king's eyes as he walked through it.

"I thought you may be undecided," he said.

I shook my head. "But why me?"

"It is as I said. I would like the chance to mend your broken heart. A heart that is cracked and ruined, Danae, is a rare thing. People speak of their broken hearts, but what they really speak of is trampled pride, rejected love. But you…" He sighed as he looked over at me.

Through the high window I saw the flame trees that grew higher than the palace, wrapped in their crimson cloaks. They leaned as though bracing themselves against the wind, their leaves fiery blazes frozen against the bleak, pale sky. The king moved toward me; that moment caged me in that prison-palace as surely as the trees I looked on were rooted to the earth.

"Will it hurt?" I asked him.

He laughed, a dry rustling laugh, and walked around so he was facing me. "You have heard the things that they say? That I have a golden touch?" He leaned forward and brushed his lips across the soft flesh under my ear. Under his touch I grew so cold and shivery, as though someone had walked over my grave. Then the feeling of being somehow detached from my body; time slipped and slid around me, my limbs as light as a butterfly wing. Feeling faint, I closed my eyes and for a moment I was not *my own* anymore – I felt like I was being pulled from dark earth. Like I was being dug up from the grave by the very person who had lightly stepped over it, just before.

Panting and gasping for air, I opened my eyes and pressed my fingers to the spot he had just kissed. It was cold and metallic. It was not flesh, but not entirely inhuman either.

"Not everything I touch is turned, Danae. I have refined this for so many years. Then you come along with your sadness and your willingness to be consumed – it is there, even if you don't notice it. You will be my living girl of gold, won't you?"

I began to weep softly, but nodded all the same. "If you will promise to help me find Bess," I replied.

He nodded slowly, slipping my dress from my shoulder and holding his hands over my belly so that I could feel their heat. "The others cried and struggled, they weren't good. It's like beef, you see? If cattle are fearful before the slaughter, it toughens the meat. The others let their fear harden them and it made them no better than lovely, useless garden ornaments. And my Stonemen, always bringing me more and more, but never the right one…"

I tried not to think of all the statues adorning the gardens, the golden women who were too many to count. Tried not to think of his lies. I turned my face upward to the breeze that blew through the window and strained to listen for the morning birdsong as he knelt before me and lowered his lips to my feet.

"Slowly, slowly," I heard him murmur, and felt my hands begin to shake. My feet became heavy and the coldness crept up my legs. I realised that he would not turn me swiftly; instead, I would feel each part as it moved to something between flesh and precious metal. But I had the thought of my spell to keep me calm, knowing that despite this slow violation, I had the magic of the rag-and-bone woman inside me.

"Do you feel it, Danae?" he whispered as he moved his hands over my thighs and his mouth over my belly. "Your flesh and your skeleton are becoming golden, soft and pliable and mine. But the rest of you is *still human* and I will keep you as my own living treasure." He left a trail of saliva from my breasts down to my navel, glistening silver on gold. My hair, my skin, my torso – he traced his hands and his lips over me, his touch, his breath re-creating me. I shivered and was dug from a long-future grave a thousand times over in the hours it took to turn me.

Only the thought of Bess and my secret spell stopped me, I think, from going mad, from giving in to my repulsion and this slow violence against me. Then, in the late afternoon light, only my face remained whole, the last of my real self atop a body I could never recognise as mine.

He stood before me, then in a quiet voice called for his doctors. Three of them – including the apothecary, who did not raise his eyes to look at me – filed in holding their little black medicine bags. The late afternoon sun shone on my face as they unpacked their instruments on the table, the oldest of them pulling out a mechanism that was about the size of a human fist, with clockwork cogs and brass curlicues. A pot of boiling liquid and another of something warm and smoky were brought in. The clockwork mechanism had valves and pipes and fine copper wires running from it.

The apothecary passed it over the steam and the smoke. It creaked into life in his hands. All three murmured in an ancient language and cast their enchantment over the mechanism, which began to beat steadily. Its rhythm filled the room with the magic that imbued it. I knew, then, what it was. It filled me with peace; it would set me free from the pain of my loss.

Under the king's steady gaze, they cut through me with their diamond-tipped instruments: I felt the unbearable pressure on my chest but, strangely, no pain. My turncoat body had become something that no longer belonged to me. Onward they cut, through fleshly, unearthly gold, then separating the soft metal ribs until they reached my heart. Organic and beating and still my own.

He walked forward, staring at me with the fervent eyes of a lover. I begged silently for it to be over quickly. I didn't scream, but they must have seen how quickly my heart beat in terror. I could smell its warmth.

The king leaned forward, his mouth mere inches away from my open chest in which my heart beat frantically, then *breathed…*

When I awoke, the surgeons and apothecary had left and I was alone with him again, the clockwork heart beating in my chest, sheathed in golden skin that had knitted together again. My heart was in his hands and he turned it this way and that in the sunset light. It was rose gold, tipped with rubies, a monstrously beautiful remnant of something that had once lived. Perfectly still, it was his prize.

The clockwork heart pumped blood through my veins and I wondered how long it would keep me alive. The king turned to me and smiled, hugged the jewelled heart to his chest and moved forward to give me his final kiss. Through the window behind him, dusk bruised the sky and I had nothing left to give but my words as he leant forward to kiss my lips.

My anger, my terror, my revulsion coursed through me, and I felt like I was on fire. I bit, hard, on his bottom lip until I tasted the copper of his blood. "I have magic of my own, my king. Did you think that I wouldn't recognise my own sister in the waters of your lake?" I hissed. It was my turn to smile. "Just an ordinary man after all."

The brand of the rag-and-bone woman on my tongue began to burn and the spell words spilled from my mouth. Words of love, words of hate, and ancient words to enslave a king. He cried out and fell to his knees, dropping his ruby-studded trophy, frozen on the spot as the words weaved their way around him. A long ago wind spun around him in a ghostly web.

"*Your* fear will make you tender to my words," I spat at him. The words of the rag-and-bone woman ran from my tongue down my throat, through my metal flesh and bone, turning it human again. It burned like fire and ice; it stung with the clean pain of deep, sharp cuts. I flexed my fingers and toes in exquisite agony.

He gagged and dirty molten gold dribbled from his lips. I watched in savage pleasure as his body began to calcify and turn to limestone, as common as the cliffs or the palace walls. I grabbed a sharp, curved blade and cut through his still-warm flesh. There – it was veined in gold and onyx, a red-purple jewel encased in a stone casket. A thing not quite beating, not quite still.

The spell swirled around the room, now beyond my control, as the canopic jars began to tremble with its force. In the crepuscular light, the king's eyes looked almost human before they, too, turned to stone.

I didn't have much time, so I wrapped his heart and the jewelled ornament that was once mine in one of the surgeon's black cloths, then grabbed the jar with Bess' lovely face carved on the lid. Her sapphire eyes stared up at me without judgement. I left him there, a harmless lump of stone turning cold as the darkness closed in, and fled through the dark and deserted halls.

* * *

"You have blood on your lips," said the rag-and-bone woman, laughing as I tried to hastily brush it away.

She held out her hand and I placed what used to be my heart in it. "The cost of your spell, as agreed," I said. She tucked it into the furs that lined the hut floor. "But what can I do with *this*?" I pointed to the cloth that held the king's heart.

"You have won it, Danae. I dare not contemplate what could happen if it were reunited with what was the king's body and will only die when you do. It must never leave your care, do you understand?"

I wished she had given me a different answer. The thought of having *it* with me forever made me shudder, but the thought of the awful things that would begin all over again if it wasn't was worse.

"And the other women in the gardens? What will happen to them?"

His words still rang in my ears. *"It toughens the meat…"* The rag-and-bone woman shook her head, and I knew then that nothing could ever bring them back to life.

"When will I stop feeling the loss of my sister? I feel the same as I did before. Even without my…"

Sighing, she reached out and touched my cheek. "That is a love that goes beyond the heart or the mind; it cannot be touched by magic or mended by the words of an old woman. It is your privilege and your burden. Everything has its price – even love."

Can we ever know the true cost?

* * *

I am an old woman now; my clockwork heart is winding down. The sacrifices Bess made for me weren't in vain: I was a healer for a long time, specialised in healing the scars left by the Stonemen. Those who had been hiding rose again after the king's death, but I refused to live in world that wasn't *after*.

In the dark of night I called to them, sent them back to the cursed place where they belonged. In the garden the Stonemen curled at the feet of the golden women or slithered into the lake where they lay. They curled around the shining statues and waited.

As the garden overgrew and fallen fruit rotted on the ground, gold bled into stone and stone into gold, marbling together until they were indistinguishable. Underneath a cloak of lichen and verdigris fungus, those still things weathered away, almost in the way that the dead should.

Bess dream-walks there sometimes, its decay comforting her.

No matter how far I wandered or what strange company I kept over the years, she was always with me. She comes to me in dreams and sometimes in waking, forever young and lovely. Her canopic jar stands on the windowsill, next to the bell jar that holds his heart. At times I wonder if I shouldn't have buried hers in a proper grave, but I could never quite bring myself to do so. So I keep them both close, wreathed in rose hips and briar thorns, but for very different reasons. Sometimes, when the wind is just so and it gusts through the window, his heart softly pulses. It has a cadence with which I am still unfamiliar, after all these years.

But when the wind blows and his heart beats, Bess sings to me from places unknown. She is soothing me still; singing to me of the darkness before dawn, of the light that burns inside us and in the cold stars above. Of golden futures and castles of sand in worlds beyond harm. Bess sings to me of the goodness that lies in the land of shadows beyond.

the psychometrist

The clips were crafted in the shape of angel wings. Each feather was finely detailed enamel, coloured indigo and pale lilac. They were backed in silver and covered with a thin layer of glass.

"Art deco. This pair is unique. They form a ladies' belt buckle – see? As objects themselves I estimate their worth at six thousand dollars," I said. My clients, a young couple who had recently bought the old property, gasped. I gave them my professional smile. "I imagine you would like to know the memory attached, before we provide the written copy and certificate of authentication? They belonged to the wife of the owner of this house. The marriage was not a good one, for she had a secret lover, who had the clips made and gave them to her before the wedding. You say you found them in a hidden box in the main bedroom? And the rest of the house was empty?"

The Schaeffers nodded, excited smiles lighting their faces.

"The wife would send one of the wings to her lover when it was safe for them to meet. He would return the wing at the meeting, and so on. It continued until she died at…" – I lightly ran my gloved fingers over the clips to ascertain that final detail – "seventy, if I'm not mistaken. She was the only owner of these, so there is no muddling of memories. That, plus the story, increases the value to $8,500."

As I packed my materials away, Mrs. Schaeffer touched my arm. I pulled away abruptly, but not before I felt her curiosity and something akin to fear jolt through me. If I am unprepared for an emotional resonance, particularly one transmitted from bare skin, it is a shock. "I would remind you, madam, that under no circumstances are you to touch me. I thought I made that clear."

"I'm very sorry, Mr. Hobgood, but, you see, there's something else that's been bothering us. We thought, since you're here…"

I composed myself. "What is it you want me to look at?"

* * *

The door to the bedroom was encased in metal, studded on all four edges with rivets. There was a large lock and bolt on the outside and no handle on the inside. The room was small, with two single beds. The wallpaper was a cheerful, flowery affair, the floor bare. Standing before the entrance, I was cold; as though winter had gotten into my bones. Something was very wrong. Even through my gloves I could sense pain, and it prickled at my fingertips. Luckily, I never value bare-handed. The buyers of the pieces I value know that they have their own feelings and don't need the memories of someone else's. What they are really after is the life of the piece itself, for the stories increase the value. With gloves I sense memory and stories, but bare skin lets the emotions through.

"We wondered why this room would have a metal door with a lock on the *outside*? Maybe you could help solve the mystery?" Her voice was hard around the edges, the tone irritating. I stepped toward the threshold and was assaulted by the sounds of children crying. The sobbing was desperately sad, almost grief-stricken. But it was muffled by fear that someone would hear. Fear of retribution.

Stepping away, I motioned for the door to be closed. Standing too close was terribly distracting, for the memories were strong. Older recollections, or gentle, non-confrontational ones feel far away, soft, out of focus, and sepia-toned. They are quite pleasant to read.

These memories, however, were not far away, not soft. Sometimes the echoes of an object's owner are so vivid, so *present* that it is difficult for me to get too close. If I allowed it, these old thoughts would run me through. Bold red, black, midnight-blue, they tasted bitter, like burnt almonds. There was no ambiguity there. They were the kind of remembrances that were wound together like rope around something rotten.

"There is some rather disturbing material here. Of course, I will be able to convey the story of it, but you may find it distressing." I tried to proceed delicately, but they both nodded to me avidly.

"The owner was a well-respected psychiatrist." I paused. The voices were strong and the colours flashed in my peripheral vision; my limbs were stabbed by short bursts of pain and my head began to ache. I moved further from the door and the voices faded, the pleas of children lingering for a moment then dying in the still air. "He was a most unpleasant man. His daughters would be locked in here as punishment. They would be tormented by him. These…*chastisements* were…unimaginably cruel. "

They smiled at one another. "This is just what we were hoping for," Schaeffer whispered to his wife. He then turned to me.

"Would you be willing to accept a further commission of a more *personal* nature?"

"I do hope you're not suggesting that I transfer the emotions from this room to you?" The thought was disquieting to say the least.

"We know that someone in your position usually doesn't do this sort of thing. But we'd pay you—" I held up my hand for them to stop. They were Drainers. Their kind usually start with watching torture porn. But once they're desensitised, it's not a huge move to sapping the pain and fear from real life horror. How such a seemingly normal couple could want to experience that was beyond me. Wasn't it enough that they had their own feelings?

I looked at them with distaste – inadequate, but the best I am able to do in such circumstances. "Not only is that highly unethical and unlawful, it is also extremely unsafe. The process puts an enormous stress on both Medium and Drainer. I do not deal in emotions and am appalled you have suggested it." I walked towards the front door.

"Mr. Wendell sends his regards, Mr. Hobgood." She caught me off-guard. It wasn't a name I expected to hear again, but it was one that made me wish I could still *hate*. The last time I had seen Wendell he was destitute and being escorted from his home. I thought I'd arranged it well enough not to encounter him again.

"Tell him he'll not receive anything else from me." I left before they had a chance to respond.

* * *

As my driver wound the car back to my home on the outskirts of the Autumn Sounds, I wondered if Katrina knew what the Schaeffers were when she referred them to me. I would be surprised if that were the case, for the area is as much her home as mine, and the inhabitants are protective of it. We value this contemplative place away from the freneticism of the city and the dark spaces of the borderlands. The leaves are always gold and red, rustling softly on branches made dark by morning fogs. Thin, crystalline patches of ice float on the edges of the water, untouched by sunlight. The sun itself hides behind the mountains or the thick grey cover of clouds.

I was unsettled that Drainers had managed to creep so far in. They usually kept close to the coast, on the Mercury Seas, where there was plenty of misery to keep them occupied.

The fact that the Schaeffers knew Wendell was even worse. I had heard rumours, over the years, that he had taken up residence by the seaside. No doubt it was there he had met the Schaeffers.

The day had made me recall my time apprenticed to him, of the day he taught me his little secret. Things I had worked hard to forget.

"The way to block emotion?" Mr. Wendell had looked down at me, his face fat and greasy like a slug. I nodded excitedly.

He leaned forward, and I recoiled, his foetid breath almost making me gag. "You must divest yourself completely of your most precious memories. No doubt you still own the object they're attached to," he sneered. Anger burned in my gut – I hated Wendell, but he was the best in the country.

"You'll need to sell it. A psychometrist's memories are highly valued and rare, as you well know." He lowered his voice to a reverential whisper. "We are like the phoenix, Hobgood. There are others like us, but only one whose talents are prized above others. You wish to take my place when I am gone, I see that in you. To do so – the reminiscences you value most will need to be drained." Had I not known better – had I though he felt *anything* – I would have sworn he took joy in my discomfort. My repulsion.

"Can't it just be cleansed?" My voice sounded small, trembling.

"It could, of course. If you're interested in mediocrity. Sacrifice is required, Hobgood." He leaned over and held my chin in his right hand.

His grip was hard, his skin clammy. It made me feel empty, like I was dying. "Just think of a life without emotions. You'll be purified. You'll be free."

I didn't know the cost.

The next day I handed him the silver pocketwatch. Curlicues and imps were etched into its surface around the "H," illuminated like a letter from an ancient text. The watch had ticked away all the important moments in my life and it terrified me to be giving him my past. But the thought of being ordinary terrified me more.

I swallowed the panic rising in my throat as he dropped a few pieces of gold into my empty hand. Payment for the measure of my life so far and my feelings forever.

"The buyer?"

He smiled, showing his sharp, yellowing teeth, then pointed to himself. Fear and horror made me light-headed and Wendell laughed as I steadied myself on the counter.

"Hobgood, even an innocent such as you must see the beauty, the *symmetry* in this. Your talent is extraordinary and that exacts a high price from you. This" – he twirled the fob chain around his forefinger – "will make you untouchable."

Even from you, I thought.

Since that day, I have known no complexities – love, fear, happiness, rage, dread – of my own. I am the best in my field, which does not allow me to feel anything. I live with my choice.

As soon as I was able, I *ruined* my former master; he made me great not realising it would mean his fall. But there *is* something left in me, cruel and deep, that needs to feel something. A pauper feeding on the scraps of men. Because I feel nothing of my own, I *crave* the feelings of other. My need, dark and dangerous, gnaws at me endlessly.

I hadn't left the Schaeffers' house quickly because I was appalled at the request. I left because I had wanted to say yes.

* * *

That night I watched from the leadlight windows, waiting for Katrina to arrive. The air was still against the gathering dark. My house is old, and the walls had whispered their tales to me when I first came here. I suffered it for long months while I saved to have the Cleaners come in. The skills of people who can clear imprints from objects and homes are prized and expensive. They weren't unpleasant memories, but it is difficult to live with that kind of thing constantly. With relief, I moved out for the two months it took to scrub the stories and the resonances from the structure of the house. I'm told that they sing them away and ingest the recollections. But Cleaners keep their secrets close and this may just be a pretty myth.

Sparsely fitted out with plain furniture and draperies with no previous owners, my house makes me think of a museum waiting to be filled. It is all high ceilings, polished floors, and space. The bridal glasses from my parents' wedding are the only trinkets I own. The goblets sit on the dark mantle over the sitting room fireplace positioned to catch the light from the setting sun. At dusk I would sit in the single white armchair in the centre of the room among the thousands of rainbow points they threw on the walls and ceiling. Their happiness dancing around me. There were no other memories of the past to fetter or disturb me.

My home is the only place I have ever known silence.

It was night when Katrina knocked on the door. She wore a long black coat, buttoned to the neck, and a black scarf around her head, pulled forward to obscure her face. The street lamps were lit, surrounded by moths bumbling their way into the brightness. Katrina was just another shadow passing through the circles of light. There was nothing to give away her identity. Discretion was crucial. I was never embarrassed about using the services of a whore, but I am a man of good reputation. People would, I imagine, harbour some doubts about my taste if they met Katrina. The more discerning of them may guess what it was that I employed her for.

I let her in and she walked straight down the hall, turning right into the room I had set aside for her visits. She knew not to linger in the other parts of the house. Not to leave remnants of herself in my home.

The single lamp in the corner cast a soft yellow light across the windowless, bare room.

Katrina stood in its centre and began to undress as I watched her. I took her scarf and hung it over one of the wrought-iron hooks on the back of the door, then watched as she unbuttoned her coat slowly, popping the tiny pearls out of their fabric loops. I knew that she would be naked underneath. My hands trembled slightly in anticipation, the most exquisite part of pleasure. As the coat parted with each loosened button, a thin line of flesh appeared, followed by the curve of her belly. She shrugged the coat off her shoulders and it fell in a dark pool at her feet.

Her body still held shadows of its former sensuality, but time had swept through her. The soft lighting couldn't camouflage Katrina's wrinkles, her leathered skin, the sag of her breasts and buttocks. She had worked until she was in her late forties, then became the madam of her own operation. The money I offered her to service me, however, had brought her back into the game at fifty-seven.

Countless men had marched across that body. It was fertile ground for me. Their longing and needs, cruelties and secrets had fossilised within her. My touch could excavate them.

Katrina provided my secret pleasure. I intended to mine her until there was nothing left.

My gloves I removed slowly; pinching the tips of the thumb, then each finger until the soft suede slipped easily over my wrists. I ran my hands over her, tracing across her shoulder and the outline of her clavicle. She was still, her black and silver-streaked hair a play of light and shadow. Fear struck through me first; I almost whimpered. Next, loneliness, which made me want to curl into a ball. I stepped away from her slightly, but didn't lift my hands from her. Rage and frustration drew me back towards her and I flexed my fingers against the desire to tighten my hands around her throat. Joy, despair, gratitude all rushed through me in waves. Katrina closed her eyes, impassive as the echoes of thousands of men pulsed through her flesh and into my hands. I was electrified, filled up as they thrilled through me. Moving around to stand behind her, I brushed her hair to one side and wrapped my arms around her body. My hands rested on her waist. I laid my head on her shoulder, my lips against the soft skin of her throat, and wept.

* * *

The house was dark after she had left. In my need for her, I had forgotten to ask about the Schaeffers. I couldn't sleep. For the first time, an encounter with Katrina had left me restless. Doubt began to creep in at the edges of my thoughts. I wasn't like the Drainers; I did not exploit people's misery. Katrina and I had a commercial arrangement. But I wanted more. I wanted what was in that room. Not for the thrill of it, but the need. The thought nibbled at my mind.

Wendell had lied. There was nothing pure or free in my life. The memories of others kaleidoscope around me or smile like long ago ancestors whose bones have turned to dust. I cloak my hands in black suede so as not to be damaged by the emotions that go with those memories, but secretly hunger to run my bare fingers over everything. There is nothing of *me* but emptiness cloaked in human flesh.

He had made me read the watch after he handed me the coins. It felt warm, its steady tick reassuring. The recollections tasted strange, like woody herbs mixed with something akin to the metallic taste of blood. I closed my eyes as everything that had been poured into the watch danced through me. The hours as my father waited until I was born; the night of my seventh birthday, when he'd given me the watch; the days of our trips to the Winterplains where the world stretched out clean and white and silent. I felt light, blissful, safe.

I had hardly opened my eyes again when Wendell hit me with his closed fist. I fell backward onto the ground, stunned. He walked slowly toward me, the look on his face vicious. It terrified me so much that I couldn't move. Straddling my chest he pinned me down, then lifted my left arm.

"Did you know that there is a direct line running from the left hand to the heart, Hobgood? Your hand is burning. Do you feel that all the way to your heart?"

He smiled as he produced a small knife from his pocket and cut the underside of my arm, just deep enough for a small stain of blood to well up, crimson and dark. I turned my head away as he brought it to his lips, cold against my flesh. I wanted to say stop, but the words stuck in my throat. As I struggled, my revulsion began dissipating. Then my fear faded into nothingness like a pale winter sky. Wendell dropped my arm, stood, and walked away without another word. It had been savage; it left me feeling nothing.

From that moment on, I was a breach waiting to be filled. And for the first time ever, taking from Katrina had not dammed that breach.

I roamed the house all night. I should have reported the Schaeffers, should have made sure that temptation was removed.

But I didn't.

* * *

I could hear the children crying. The Schaeffers were in the kitchen, at the other end of the house. I would read the door privately, and transfer the emotions to them later.

I stood for a long time. This is wrong, I thought. You could lose everything.

It would all be for nothing, I argued, knowing that either way I would lose. I struggled as the weeping filled my ears.

–To feel. No one will ever know. The children are gone, grown up and far away. At least, in some way, their suffering will help you.

–They suffered. You are going to take that suffering for yourself. You're no better than the Drainers.

–I'm nothing like them. They're parasites and I have a true need.

I removed my gloves, roughly, before I could change my mind. My legs spasmed, my stomach cramped, but I moved towards the door. It creaked on its hinges.

The voices shouted and the metal radiated heat as if in response. I hesitated, then pushed my hands hard against the trapped, burning memories. Misery pressed on my chest and I gasped. The horror cut through to my spine. Pain shot through the nerves in my hips and my limbs stung. My palms were fixed to the door as surely as if an electric current ran from it through me.

Colours exploded in front of my eyes. The stench of rotting fruit filled my nose and mouth, making me retch. Violins screeched and funereal drums beat across my ribs. Somewhere, someone screamed himself raw. I realised it was me. The acrid taste of ashes mingled with the salt of my own tears.

Every emotion, every feeling, every hurt, every ache, every agony, was *mine*.

It all stopped, silent, the air frozen. A silver knife flashed against the doctor's throat, scarlet stained the child's hand. Then a soft green light, fading to watery lily-white. The terror dissipated and I was filled with overwhelming relief, clean as ocean air.

Collapsing, I tried to get my bearings. I felt hands grip my arms tightly and drag me into the darkened hallway, eager for their prize. Fevered anticipation lit the Schaeffers' eyes. I tried my professional smile and beckoned them closer. They sat before me and I watched them bind their left wrists together with white silk, according to my instructions.

"This isn't how Wendell does it," she whispered.

"I think you'll find my technique a little more refined," I rasped. From my pocket I drew a tapered candle and silver lighter. The wick caught and the tiny flame danced as I held it over their upturned left palms. The burns I made on their wrists were entry points. Neither of them flinched. The flame died. I put my mouth over the blistering skin, soft as a lover's kiss.

They held their breath, waiting for the room's secrets; instead I poured into them all my own emptiness, the void of which I had been composed for so long. They tried to pull away, but I held tight. I held on for my life.

It seemed I swam up from the depths. Dark green, murky water cleared as light began to filter through. With a final kick I broke the surface, felt gentle warmth on my skin and breathed in sweet air.

The lights in my clients' eyes guttered. Everything went black.

* * *

When I woke again, I was in the hospital. Uncertain recollections of soft voices and kind hands lifting me flitted briefly, and the image of the Schaeffers fading like ghouls into the shadows. It disappeared as swiftly. The room was clean, uncluttered. Wintry sunlight poured through the window, and beyond the glass stretched the Winterplains. Snow and ice as far as I could see, broken only by the silhouettes of naked trees and the last of the nightbirds swooping under the morning sky. I *had* heard of this place before, its location due to the delicate condition of its patients.

I turned at the sound of someone shifting carefully in a chair to my left. Katrina's faded blue eyes stared at me, her silver hair loose across her shoulders. She touched my face gently, all sorrow and regret.

"I didn't know," she said. I nodded, letting her sadness, her relief envelop me.

Thundering hooves drew my attention back to the window. Ice horses danced past, frozen ground cracking under their stride, the low sun melting flecks of water from their manes.

When I turned back, I saw her tears. Taking her hand, I pressed her palm to my lips. She tasted of the truth.

And more: anxiety, affection, relief. Love? Not the emotional imprints of past men, but her own feelings, given as a gift. They spun from her, web-like, beautiful in their complexity.

Words fluttered in my throat and I gave a small smile. Answering her, another feeling, skittering and new. Happiness, I realised. My own.

sundark and winterling

Sundark awoke to rain drumming on the windowpane and dripping from the eaves. In the street below, the footsteps of early risers splashed along the cobbles. None paused outside her house; the house that was once the dragon, Winterling. It was almost as though most of the people had all but forgotten it was there; a splash of jewels and dragon skin against the shadowy gothic spires and crooked mansions that spread through the old district. They were used to living alongside the fae, so many people thought the music that rilled from the roof and rained down from the eaves on moonlit nights was just a clever trick, when they bothered to notice it at all.

It was no trick. In the grey morning, Sundark listened for Winterling's song, but there was nothing but the patter of raindrops and the faint shouts of the early market opening down by the pier. Then, snatches of conversation between two of her charges floated down from the rooftop:

"I don't think she'll ever come back." Gutterblood's tone was obstinate.

"Nonsense," Bellibone replied. "How else will songs be written, poetry set to Winterling's glorious notes, if she stays away forever?"

Sundark smiled and pulled her mind up towards them, hovering at their shoulders as they sat on the edge of the roof, their feet dangling over the edge. Gutterblood and Bellibone were two of the word-ghosts – the *erutisi* – who haunted the city. They were the fragile echoes of forgotten words who had found refuge with Sundark, the fae charged with guardianship of forgotten words, lost language. As small as children and nebulous as mist, erutisi faces flickered and changed constantly, shaped and reshaped by all the mouths that had ever spoken them. While the other erutisi awoke in their nooks and crannies within the house, Gutterblood and Bellibone's chatter comforted Sundark in the face of what this day meant. Of what she had to do, now that a year and a day had passed since Winterling's death.

Gutterblood sighed. "But we will have to learn to look after ourselves—"

Bellibone silenced him with a stern look. "The house is all we need for now. She has to avenge Winterling's death, now the mourning period is done. I was there, you know. When it happened." They both began to swing their feet excitedly. Ghosts they may have been, but words are *always* enthralled by a good story. "After the fae-king Rakmore had slain all the other dragons in the country, he came for Winterling. Even though he was the lover of Rakmore's sister, Sundark. Even though it was the day of the lovers' wedding, on the winter solstice…"

The image carved through Sundark and she pulled her mind downwards, back into the room. The downpour grew heavier. Winterling had loved to fly in storms, whipping through heavy clouds, the rain on his scales ringing like far-away bells. Against the grey sky, he was a flash of dark light, a flame in an ocean of ash. His music came from the elements hitting his body, and his mood as he cut through the air. The thunder was his beat and bass, the crack of lightning the crash of cymbals. The music that sparked off Winterling on those fragile days was a fierce fight against the storm, which then faded to melancholia as the storm marched on.

But that was in the days before dragon-music was outlawed; before they were slain and their bodies burned on pyres that hissed and sung funereal dirges as the scales burned; before Winterling's brother discarded his own skin, shifting into his man-shape forever and eloping with Rakmore's wife. Rakmore: Sundark's brother and her bane.

"Good morning, Winterling," Sundark said under the sound of the rain. The house sighed gently in return. She rose and began to get ready for the day, wanting to remain as long as possible in that room lined with the soft moss and basalt rocks from her tribe's land. Who knew when she would return?

The house sighed again, this time a little mournfully.

"You know that I have to leave – but you must also know that I'll be back, don't you?"

There was no answer. She looked out of the arched window, framed by the smaller of his ribs, watched as the cobblestones and buildings began to steam as the morning sun hit the soaked city. Smoke curled on the back of the early morning breeze; it reminded Sundark of a funeral pyre, and she pushed away thoughts of the great fire she had used to render Winterling's flesh from his bones. It had been worth it though, hadn't it? The house was a glorious and sturdy construction. The triple spurs from each of his hind legs were used to anchor the foundations deep into the earth; the vertebrae of his snake-like spine for the wall struts, fibula and tibias for the rafters; the larger of his ribs formed the curve of the roof and walls. The spires topping the house were his talons and claws.

"I know that it's been a poor substitute, but at least we've been together this last year."

The house that used to be Winterling didn't respond.

* * *

As she left the bedroom, a cape of raven feathers, each with its own gleam of violet and emerald light, waited for Sundark at the bottom of the staircase; a dark memory against the pearly whiteness of the balustrade made from Winterling's teeth.

"Gifts, my love? This was my wedding mantle, as you well know, and I put it on your pyre." The last time she had worn it, Sundark had flown across the skies with Winterling, a dark raven and a flash of bright song-scales over snowy peaks and the vast city. Only a few hours later, those same scales shone crimson with Winterling's blood.

The feathers shook irascibly, as though ridding themselves of water or ash. The other erutisi drifted through the entrance hall, whispering to one another and pointing at the cape. Gutterblood and Bellibone looked down from the landing above.

Market smells of new cut flowers, animal manure, and spices flooded through the window; morning birds called through the mist outside as she walked over to the cape. He had made it whole again, despite the tearing and ripping from being chased, held, made to watch as Rakmore brought down his sword. Despite her trying to burn away those memories.

"Objects of love should be happy memories," Bellibone called down.

"Put in on," the others whispered.

The feathers were fine and silken beneath her fingertips, the oil-colour speaking of soaring and open skies and song. The erutisi giggled as she shed her clothes then threw the cloak around her shoulders. Preening, fluffing and smoothing like a dove grooming itself in the sun, it fitted itself to Sundark *just so*. She swung her hips, smiled at the way the feathers brushed her ankles, at how her bones felt light and hollow with the memory of flight winging through them.

"Thank you," she said. In reply, the front door and those to Sundark's bedroom, the parlour, and all the ground floor rooms disappeared, leaving behind smooth walls.

Sundark laughed. "Very well, upstairs it is then."

She ascended the winding staircase, trailing her hand over the balustrade. On the second floor, the same; nothing but adobe walls, splashed here and there with the rough jewels gifted to Sundark and Winterling on their wedding day. Sundark leaned against one of the walls, felt it move beneath her. She rested her forehead against it, in the same way she would lean against him in the sunlight as he stretched out across pebbled beaches or in the desert ravines after his flight. His dragon-shape, his true shape, so different from her own always fascinated her. Being close to him had never been close enough; so much so that she had often thought she would like to unpick his edges, as though de-seaming a garment, and crawl inside him. After his death, she had done just that.

Sundark continued to the uppermost storey, the erutisi watching her with their strange, changeling faces. "Winterling will keep you safe while I'm gone." She could almost smell her brother's blood. He may have had revenge in his heart when he murdered Winterling and his brothers, but Sundark had taken her full mourning period to nurture the revenge and hatred simmering inside her, to cool and ferment it into a poison more potent than nightshade. Only a fool kills in rage; only a coward punishes the innocent as well as the guilty.

Gutterblood beckoned to her from the top of the staircase. On the third floor were the map room and the tiny staircase to the roof. Both doors were open. At the top of the stairs lay a second gift from the house; shoes of bone, moonbeam bright with heels like scythes. Sundark's breath caught in her throat as she turned one of the shoes delicately in her hands. Shards from a mermaid's tail supported the sole; the ridged fibulas of satyrs had been carved as the vamp; phoenix wing-bones, like thin flames, licked the shoe's quarter.

She stepped into the left, then the right. "These belong to the shapeshifters of the Bitter Sea. How did you... *Where* did you get these from?"

Gutterblood sank into the wall, reappearing a moment later looking faintly harried. "He says they are to remind you that there is more in this world than revenge and loss. There are beautiful things unexplained – there is life! But if you must go after Rakmore, you are not going alone. You have allies."

As she walked to the map room, the heels sparked on the floor, the power of earth, fire, and sea sheathing her feet.

* * *

The globe, covered in fine vellum and kept shut tight with an ornate brass lock, was small enough to fit into Sundark's palm. Cloaked in raven's feathers, shod in shoes of bone, she stood in the centre of the map room with a sinking heart at Winterling's third gift. She looked up at the maps lining the walls, with their ever-changing boundaries and cruel seas. The two huge globes that stood to shoulder height and marked the worlds of humans and fae revolved slowly. Here she had the power to re-map all the worlds, remake new language from old with her fragile erutisi, but nothing could change the hollow space in her life that his death had left; the hollow space of an unlived life. And now this.

"You want me to use a memory box?" Anger shook her, for she knew what he intended her to do. "I store my memories of you in here and as soon as I leave this house – you! – it will be as though you never existed to me. I will forget Rakmore and I... I will never find *you* again!"

On the wall maps, on the shore of the Bitter Sea, two fae appeared with armies behind them; armies that cut each other down until the sea ran red.

"His hate makes him ruthless and he will keep killing anyway — because of me or in spite of me."

The figures on the wall faded and house fell silent.

"And what about all the forgotten words, whom I am charged with guarding? They are like my children…"

The walls dented and morphed into recesses and spaces that would fit the erutisi. The windows sealed over, making the room snug and dark.

"I know you will look after them." She turned the memory box over in her hand, feeling its weight. "What do you think they would have been like? Our children, I mean."

Bright flames began to blaze in the enormous fireplace. In their centre, the shapes of three children, with long, wild hair like Sundark's, danced and ran about. Great dragon wings unfurled from their backs and they flew upward, skimming the chimney then coming to rest in the grate. The flames crackled and sang in the voices of their unborn children. Of orange and white flame, the children stopped and turned toward Sundark, their intensity stinging her eyes.

One last flare then the fire died, leaving behind grey ashes and the shadows of the three serpentine children branded on the fireplace wall. Sundark dropped to her knees and scooped up handfuls of the still-warm ash, rubbing it onto her face and hands. It streaked her skin the dull silver of loss.

A little copper key appeared on the floor beside her. Picking up the memory box, Sundark fitted the key to the brass lock. She opened it, held it to her mouth, and began to whisper into it as the house opened its windows to the sunlight and morning breeze.

* * *

Sundark opened the door to the outside for the last time. She stepped out, being careful to move gently in her sharp shoes. The erutisi followed, chasing one another and scattering like leaves across the blue curves of the roof.

Of all the wonder and beauty of the house — its ever-changing rooms, sturdy structure of bone, its moods and magic — Sundark loved the roof most of all. It was Winterling's hide, carefully removed and cleaned, and stretched over the frame of his bones. Shaped like waves or rolling dunes, it gleamed azure and indigo, undulating gently as the sun hit it or the house settled or tried to soothe his wife.

Just as music had rained from Winterling's skin during his lifetime, the roof sang under moonlight and sunshine, storm and spring wind. Sundark would often stretch herself out up there on starry nights, shut her eyes, and imagine that she was curled next to him as he sang her to sleep. On those nights, the roof would sing of the summer and winter solstices, the two days and nights each year that Winterling and his brothers would take their human form. Even in his man-shape, his skin had had an otherness that drew her to him. Scale and flesh and skin, the exquisite pain of his music running across her. Both skin-hungry and ravenous after the long months of waiting; then the waiting again until he could next take his man-shape. The welts he left on her would remain weeks after the longest day and the longest night had each passed. When she touched one or her clothes pressed against them, the stinging pain spoke to her of his love.

That morning, she lay in a Sundark-shaped depression and pressed her ear to the shining cerulean scales. Each one lifted and settled at her touch, crooning a lover's tune of farewell.

Far below, over the market and city sounds, came drumbeats and the marching of many feet. Sundark sat up, alarmed at their unfamiliarity. The dragon-skin fell silent. The erutisi crowded together and looked to their guardian. She put her finger to her lips in a shushing motion and crawled over to the edge, peering into the cobbled streets below.

A king's guard of thirteen men marched towards the house and fanned out around it. Before them, Rakmore walked with his warrior's stride, smiling grimly. He stopped before the front door.

"One year and one day, Sundark. But I've saved you the trouble of coming for me. All you have to do is walk out your front door."

* * *

The erutisi gathered around Sundark, patting her gently on the back and stroking her hair. She had not expected this. She peered over the edge again; below, Rakmore appraised the house, the hatred on his face clear.

Even now, the betrayal of his wife with Winterling's brother consumed him. He reached out and touched the front door. It hissed at him and he laughed drily. His men drew their axes and stood to attention.

"You have two minutes, sister. If you aren't before me in that time, we will come in after you."

Sundark drew back from the edge and beckoned the oldest thirteen of her charges to her. Their ancient faces flickered and changed, but their eyes never left her. They fanned out around her as she stood, arms outstretched, the feathers gleaming in the sun. Gutterblood, Bellibone, and all the others huddled by the door.

Mouth wide open in a silent scream, Sundark threw her head back as the thirteen erutisi spun around her, fast and faster still. They thinned like mist until they were no more than a curl of smoke; Sundark drew them towards her with a deep breath, inhaling them until the air was clear again.

Forgotten language, muscular and elegant, rippled under her skin. The roof sang out, a war cry that stilled the city and made Rakmore and his men shiver. Standing on the eaves, Sundark's shape filled the sky. The toes of her shoes of bone hung over the edge; then a little further. With arms outspread, she fell through the air towards the street below, towards her brother.

Shoes of bone became razor talons. The feathered cape stretched, then shrank, shaping itself into its avian form so it was no longer the fae Sundark falling but the raven Sundark swooping and flying among the invaders. One after another Rakmore's men drew their silver broadswords, striking at Sundark, but she was too nimble for them. She flew upwards, opened her beak. And the old language she had consumed found voice again. They were words no longer recognised by any fae or human mind or tongue. Ancient, keening cries, thirteen in all, fell from the raven's throat and flew towards Rakmore's guard of thirteen men. As the men cried out, the words made a home of their mouths. They buried themselves deeper; unfamiliar in their throats, the old words choked them.

Rakmore spun around, eyes wide as the men of his guard asphyxiated and dropped, lifeless, to the ground. Sundark dived toward him, her claws cutting deep into his upper arm as he ducked away from her. With a guttural, raging shout he drew his axe and swung it at the house. Dragonfire spewed out from its doors and windows. Rakmore dropped the axe and fell backward as the air filled with the smell of burnt hair and singed flesh.

As pain distracted him, Sundark dived again. She flapped her wings and shifted her weight as she attacked. He could not grab hold of her. Her talons gouged his cheeks and he screamed a terrible scream as she pecked and pecked at his face. She flew upward again, feet drenched in his blood and her beak gore-slicked. Rakmore held his hand to his ruined face, his now-empty eye-socket, and reached for his axe again.

More footsteps as his first battalion ran through the streets towards the house. The windows and doors continued to flame, forcing all the soldiers backwards. Sundark flew once, twice around the eaves, darting to avoid the arrows aimed at her. The wind began to blow fierce from the west and it caught under her. She flew upwards and to the east, towards the distant, frozen mountains, leaving the city so far behind it was as though it had never existed.

* * *

Far below Sundark, the green of the lowlands had given way to rocky foothills, then the glaciers and snow drifts of the hinterlands and high mountains. The late sun glittered on the white landscape, turning it rose-gold – the colour of Winterling's fire – driving her brother back. He and his men would have left the city by now, for he couldn't kill Winterling twice. Rakmore would follow her, but she wouldn't give him the chance to find her first. Not again.

More ravens joined her, dipping and wheeling in the cold air. A storytelling of ravens could be just as good as an army, in the right hands. She would hunt him on stealthy wings.

A small shadow flitted across the glacier below then disappeared in the gloaming. Flying lower, it reappeared. An erutisi, hardly more than steam, was making her way up the mountain. Sundark landed and took her usual form again. The erutisi stared, then raised a hand to her own chest. "Mab," she croaked.

Sundark smiled and held out her hand. Silently, they walked across the ice and settled into one of the high, dark caves above. There would be more erutisi willing to sacrifice themselves, more ravens as fierce and black as burning pitch. But the taste of Rakmore's blood had not cured Sundark of her longing. With Mab by her side and mountain ravens cawing at the last of the sun, she pined for Winterling and her charges, to remake the world with language reformed.

As night closed in, she pulled her mind back to the house that was once Winterling, gently moving as a shifting breeze past Gutterblood, Bellibone, and the other erutisi. She was connected to those forgotten words as though by a fine silver thread, and they felt her with them, across the frozen distance between them.

"I think she wants us to go to the map room," Gutterblood said.

So the many erutisi crept inside, and whispered as one to the enormous globe in the centre of the room. It opened with a leathery creak and Bellibone reached inside to pull out the little vellum globe lying at the very bottom. She held it up and they all quietened. Like a far-away bell or the shushing of waves under an autumn moon, *something* inside it sang and recited poetry, muttered dirges and laughed with light happiness.

"I remember what that felt like," said Gutterblood sadly. "To be alive and heard and remembered. How has she…?"

Bellibone laughed, realising what Sundark had done. "She is far cleverer than Rakmore or Winterling. A guardian of lost language knows the art of words right back to their beginnings. She knows how to restrain us or make us sing, even knows how to find us from far away. It's not her memories in here."

Bellibone held the memory box up to her ear and listened. Ephemeral Sundark hovered at her side, tugging and weaving the silver string of connection so that Bellibone would understand.

"Inside is Sundark's *own* language, my dears. To be kept safe until she is ready to claim it again. To go out into the world mute is her sign of mourning and a promise that she will return. So that her words and his music can come together again and be more than what they are by themselves. Just as they would have been, had he lived."

Even Gutterblood sighed happily. For Sundark there was still revenge, but there was also something waiting for her *after*, and she would find her way back to it with her shoes of bone carving rivers of words in her wake.

In the darkness, the erutisi fell asleep to the sounds of Sundark's hidden language. And as they slept, they dreamed of a raven flying high over snowy peaks; of stories made not of words, but of pearls and lucent jewels strung on indigo silk; of Sundark lying on the dragon-skin roof as though cradled by a lover.

Far above, the roof sang softly under the slow path of the stars, its notes falling through the windows and slipping through the little globe's brass lock to dance with the words inside, in the hope of Sundark's return to Winterling, in the shape of songs yet to be sung.

husk and sheaf

Spring had stretched the daylight hours and dried the damp-weather rot in my hands by the time the old woman, Emmeline, began visiting the orange grove. By then, I knew enough to see she wasn't well. I had been placed in the grove to scare away the mynahs pecking incessantly at the fruit. At first, I couldn't remember being made, or recall the feeling of the hands that sewed my body and my clothes. Who was it who stuffed me full so I plumped out like a real man?

I was much more than an ordinary scarecrow though, all rags and lopsided limbs. It wasn't straw or old newspaper inside me. The tokens that shape me are the memories of others. Dried lavender, tickets stubs from concerts and train journeys, remnants of wedding veils, locks of hair from mourning rings. Even a tiny bird's nest brought home by a child for his ailing mother sitting in the centre of my chest. Carefully stowed cogs from music boxes and wind-up toys served as my ballast.

I'm the only memory-keeper there is.

It's the old letters – some only fragments, some pages and pages long – that made me who I am, the words flowing through me akin to blood. I was their guardian and the tales coursing through me were my teachers. At the close of each day, I was *more* than I had been the day before.

So when Emmeline arrived, I was curious about all these things that comprise human lives. She was so old that her mind had started to slip and she mumbled to herself, pallid eyes staring into the distance. Occasionally, snatches of her sentences reached me and those snippets awoke the words inside me, making them sing and soar. Making me feel and think and *know*. The sweetness was tantalisingly brief and left me craving.

When she stopped, I demanded more, but it made her weep. I brushed away her tears with the edge of my coat, then I tried pleading with her, but that was beyond her way of thinking. I sifted through the words running through me, to find the right way to seek more. None were quite right, until I found a letter between old friends…

Penny for your thoughts? I whispered to Emmeline as the orange blossoms swirled around her in the breeze. Their scent, sharp citrus and sweet pollen, made me think of a long ago wedding feast of wild boar stew studded with pomegranate seeds, eaten in a summer orchard.

She smiled as, from the open tips of my disintegrating fingers, I shook a shiny copper coin and pressed it into her hand.

I smiled back and clumsily stroked her hair, silver and fine as a cobweb. The days, years, decades that had woven through her fluttered under my fingertips. Time is its own sweet song; dirge, waltz, sonata, a lonely piano in the dark hours. It tasted just as time always has. Like mist on a cold morning, carrying the promise of far-away snow and woodsmoke from cosy hearths, but fleetingly insubstantial.

Emmeline slowly handed her past over to me. Piece by sweet piece. Once she had someone to listen, her mumbling dissipated. In a voice that might have once been musical she reminisced – walking the streets of the dark city, that smelled of cigarettes and waffles, with her lover; a homeless woman singing hymns in a subway tunnel, her voice chasing Emmeline around corners and down stairs; black cats slinking through cemetery groves and white ones curled on cracked leather chairs in an ancient library.

All the while I stroked her hand, its skin paper-fine, and listened while she unburdened herself. Those memories were the marrow of life, sating me long enough to smile, never enough to be truly full. All through the spring and summer I listened, until she had nothing left for me to take.

That last day, Emmeline's words faded and she fell into a gentle doze. In the late afternoon sun, I relished her thoughts that were like aged wine, brined olives, slightly soured milk.

All spring and summer I listened, for the price of a penny. A coin to pay the Boatman to cross the silver river that tastes of stars; to go to the foggy shore that smells of everything *but* time. The shore that I can never know.

I left her in the orange grove, clutching her penny and drifting in and out of sleep. The last to listen to her, the last to understand. I left her there, hollowed, unencumbered. Free.

That night, I crept away, to the banks of the river that ran black and sluggish across its mossy bed. Yellowish moonlight silhouetted the trees and the strange shapes that lined the embankment. In the gloom, those lumpen forms were a silent warning. I shuffled towards the closest one, stopping short as its faded cotton shirt – clearly once identical to my own – became clear.

Scarecrows, frozen where they stood, in varying states of decay. Dozens of them, just like me. Only they were so still, with not even a forgotten sentence to breathe life into them. The night breeze scattered scraps of parchment from the split seams of one propped against a tree. Water-stained, the ink was spider-webbed across the paper's surface, the words now illegible.

On the far bank, the mouse-nibbled remains of another reclined, forever sleeping. The closest one with coat still bottle-green and torso intact crouched as though looking at its reflection. I sat beside it, watching the water ripple and distort the reflected night sky.

Creature of star-flecked night, chasing a hollow moon, and ever-ebbing tides... A memory uncurled in me. A memory of my own, richer and more real than the borrowed ones. Of Emmeline, floating downriver on a raft of sticks and autumn leaves. Barely alive and waiting for me. The scarecrows scattering the bank stared blankly at me. It felt like an accusation. Or a premonition. I shivered.

They were *me*. Previous incarnations, filled and emptied and left to decay on the riverbank. It was Emmeline who had made me and Emmeline who would unmake me again and again and again. We had been here dozens of times before, her and I. Bound together in an endlessly repeating dance.

I felt her before I saw her, reclined on the raft as it rounded the bend, hair fanned out like mist. In her outstretched palm, my penny glinted in the moonlight. The night smelled of autumn – cider apples and ash trees felled for firewood – but of putrefaction, as well. The raft bumped into the bank. Her chest barely rose and fell as the last of her breath in this life wheezed in and out.

Penny for your thoughts, she croaked.

Not a question, but a command that tugged the stories inside me towards her. I began to walk forward, recollections of those dozens of lifetimes that I had lived before reminding me of what would come next:

Taking the coin and popping it in my mouth, its copper like blood on my tongue.

Lifting her from the raft and walking with her into the river, the currents she has ensorcelled embracing us, dragging us under.

The future radiance of unborn stars swirling around us as the water rips the memories from me, flooding them back into her.

Emmeline's wrinkles receding, hair becoming thick and dark, her eyes bright and cruel.

I was her memory-keeper, the crucible for her phoenix-magic. I would slowly be emptied into an unthinking, unfeeling poppet and the last thing I would see is her beautiful, young face smiling at me before everything darkened and died. In my first lifetime, decades before, I had known no better and simply let her wash me away. But every time after that, I fought, the river churning around us. Each time a little harder, with the weight of memory – of taste and smell and story – behind me. Every time, she had won.

This time…a coin and a short, borrowed life were not enough to buy my submission. I took the coin from her palm and placed it over her rictus grin instead.

Her clawed fist clamped over my wrist, pulling me towards the raft, stronger than she should have been, so close to death. I slipped in the mud and fell towards her.

This is destiny, my paper-man. Her nails dug into me and I felt light-headed. Compliant, almost. Inside me though, the letters shifted. The words stirred. They didn't want to belong to her either. She struggled against the soft rot of my hand and the soft insistence of the stories inside me as they pulled away from her.

You can't give all this, Emmeline, and not expect that we will want more.

Her eyes widened at the sound of my voice and her grip loosened, for just a moment. I stepped back, ripping my arm away from her. My hand, the fabric finally worn through, stayed in hers. Tiny pieces of paper fell from my severed wrist. The words, viscous and shining, bled into the night. They swam in the darkness and disappeared on updrafts into the world beyond her reach. She rasped a scream, the coin clanking against her teeth, tried to rise from the raft as her skin withered and desiccated. The river flowed swiftly and called for payment of its own. The inky current rose, waterlogging the raft, dragging her down and away.

Far away, a train whistle blew and unseen animals rustled through their nocturnal lives. With an old coat-ribbon I staunched the word-bleed from my wrist and left that graveyard of the forgotten, walking downstream towards the open shore.

Of the stories and memories of others I may be made, but this lifetime is mine.

This story is mine alone.

the cartographer's price

"That's the only piece that's not for sale," I tell the stranger who wears a coat the colour of a shadow. At least once a week, a traveller or collector or some other poor soul asks about the map. It hangs on the wall behind the glass-topped counter, behind me, so I don't need to watch its constantly changing lines, or the strange shadows that fall across it. I'm used to it by now, but it doesn't mean that I like it.

The stranger just smiles, taps his fingers on the countertop. The ruby eyes of the skull ring adorning his middle finger sparkle, catching the light of the gas lamps and early evening glow. Unlike the others, he doesn't offer me *more than a fair price* or make empty threats to scare me into handing it over. Just smiles a little cunningly, like a rat with a gold tooth.

He looks around at the shelves crammed with stuffed, glassy-eyed foxes and owls, leather-bound books with print so tiny I sell golden magnifiers with them, and faded, sepia-toned world globes centuries old.

"Not just a cartographer then?"

Now it's my turn to smile. "On the contrary, sir, I deal exclusively in maps. They just may not be the type that you are accustomed to."

The breeze blows the scent of cinnamon and stewing meat through the open doorway. The stuffed foxes lift their noses ever so slightly, whiskers twitching. My customer raises his eyebrows, but says nothing.

"Permit me to demonstrate," I say, motioning him to hold out his hand, palm upwards. I pick up a silver-dipped magpie's skull, its beak polished to an obsidian shine, and place it in his hand. The skull is very still, the sort of stillness that comes from listening intently. Then – it swings to the left, the right, back to the left until it faces southwest. Opening its beak, it chirps out directions to Snow's Reach. A place of ravens and shapeshifters and death, I wonder what business the stranger has there.

"Fascinating," he concedes, his eyes shining. "But there is only one map that I'm after. It is one of a kind and it hangs on the wall behind you."

He puts down the skull and places his hand over mine. The flesh is work-roughened, strong, but gentle enough to feel kind. His presence is unsettling, but he has an air of *possibility* about him. It is something that is sorely lacking in Rorkenbach, with the city's soldiers patrolling the streets, footfalls like thunder as they march another unfortunate to his execution.

"I know it isn't for sale. Such an object must stay put until a worthy owner comes to claim it, no?"

I pull my hand away and move over to the copper samovar that holds hot tea brewed with orange zest and rosebuds and a tiny pinch of sea salt that blows in on the wind whipping up from the docks. I pour a cup for myself and another for the stranger.

"You know cartography lore then. More than most. Then you must also know that the only way to succeed—"

"Is to tell you the true story of its origin," he finishes.

This is a lot more dangerous than it sounds. "And you will also know that the penalty for a false story is death?"

All my maps, in their various shapes, seem to hold their breath as I silently plead for the stranger to leave. Even if I want to be merciful to a false storyteller, the map will not let me. It is a hateful, dangerous thing, full of capricious moods and misleading information. I do not want to have to dispatch yet another soul who has decided to gamble with his life. Six is more than enough. I had hoped, with each one, that they would be true. That is the strange thing about maps such as this – any one of hundreds of stories about their beginnings could be true, depending upon the direction the teller is coming from. And where they intend to go.

So I had hoped, fruitlessly, that as each of those six had begun, they might not only take away the hateful thing for good, but their story might also bring me closer to finding Nico again. I am silly enough to hope for the same thing a seventh time.

"You're sure then?" I ask, a queasy mix of anticipation and dread churning in my stomach. He nods, settles himself into the worn green chaise lounge that is an unfurling portrayal of the whole history of Rorkenbach, and sips his tea. As I shut the door and set the sign to "Closed," I nod to my fellow merchants in the lane who stand under the amber sunset, setting up for the night trade. Any one of those scoundrels and miscreants could be a spy, and I hope that the stranger has not brought trouble on me just by walking through my door.

I perch on the end of the lounge, shivering a little despite the warmth of my tea.

"This shop wasn't always yours, was it? Or always a cartographer's?" he begins. "It used to belong to a Balladliner, the only one seen in these parts for some three hundred years."

I close my eyes, remembering Nico and the music she made in the lonely hours between midnight and dawn. It would trill across the fen, wind around the wooden piers and sweep through the stone laneways and alleys, making people wonder just what its recipient had paid to Nico in return.

"You knew her, I think?" my guest asks.

I nod.

"No one knows where the Balladliners come from. The northern lands the sunlight never touches? Descended from the sirens and sailors that were man enough for them to keep close for a short while? Me, I think they are from beyond the borders of this world, dead lands where women weep themselves into stone and the cost of those tears is far greater than any that we could imagine. But what would an old pirate like me know?" He winks and, although I am far too cynical to actually blush, a giggle bubbles out from me.

"I don't know that anyone recalls when the Balladliner, Nico, arrived, or for how long she traded here. But they all remember her music, made on her strange instruments and sung from the balladlines on her flesh. For Balladliners don't sing with their voices. Her body was covered in scars, new and old, reopened and scarred all over again. All except her face and hands, where they say she kept her private music. Those scars were the balladlines of her body and musical notes bled from fresh wounds whenever she agreed to a trade. Harmonies born of opal tears and mandalas of unearthly voices gave birth to the compositions that lived beneath her skin. When Nico sailed from beyond the borders of this world, across the Bitter Seas, the music found shape and married itself to her cells." For the first time, the stranger's face is grave.

"Every song was a sacrifice. Some were obvious. The shanty she gave to the fishermen in exchange for the mermaid tied to their mast, ready to sell to Rorkenbach's soldiers for meat or Professor Finnegan for his museum, had belonged to her own mother. The day she sung at dawn to hold back the rains that threatened to flood the streets left her pale as though she'd been bled by those quack doctors' leeches."

The map behind the counter sighs and rustles irritably. It isn't a good sign. But my guest just laughs, dismisses it with a wave of his hand.

"Temperamental, isn't she?" he says.

"Almost as impatient with digression as she is intolerant of lies," I reply. I am beginning to like him and it's always more difficult to get rid of the ones with whom I feel an affinity.

"Where was I? Ah, sacrifices. Now, the more serious ones. Like how you came to be in her service, for example." He whispers, soft like spring rain, but it stills everything. The night. The map. Me.

"Tell me, how did you come to be in the commander's...entourage?"

My cup rattles in the saucer. I put it down and clasp my hands, so he can't see them shaking. "That's not part of the story."

"Of course it is! A story is a little give, a little take, a compact between teller and listener. Just like a song. What the listener brings to it is, perhaps, the most important part of all. And you are the very maker of that map, are you not? The commander's cartographer, famed for her depictions of this world and places beyond. Of lands undiscovered and things unspoken—"

"Please," I beg him, "if anyone here gets wind that I am anything more than a mere trader..."

"I have no intention of revealing you to anyone," he says, "only to be true and complete. If I am not, I will pay for it with my life."

From its place on the wall, the map asserts its dominance in this little, cramped shop. The notes of its own canticle fill the room. Oceans crashing on the shore, icebergs creaking under green-lit winter skies, airships lifting from the highest peaks to follow the secret, ever-changing paths the map holds close. She agrees with the stranger that I should take part in his story and I am oddly relieved.

"The commander was my father." The word still doesn't sit comfortably on my tongue. "He was not a loving parent, it's fair to say. Indifferent, at best, unless there was something he needed from you. When he discovered my talent with maps…" I shrug, preferring not to go over the things that seem a lifetime ago.

The stranger nods. "Nico gave the commander the last song from her old world in exchange for you. That balladline ran down her right-hand side, from armpit to hip. She used it just that once."

"I treated her for weeks afterwards," I tell him, remembering how her body had not seemed to *want* to heal. "A cartographer needs more strings to her bow than just drafting and drawing, in order to make the most unique of maps. I saw that wound and I know the sacrifice she made." But I still wonder if it was for me or for the chance to obtain the map that hangs on the wall. For it, too, had belonged to the commander. It is my most exacting work and the one that still haunts me.

"There was a connection between you and Nico, a simpatico. She exchanged the song for *you* and let him leave here that night with the map."

Remembering the night we first crossed paths still makes me smile. "It was in this very shop that we met. It was a proper Balladliner's shop then, filled with harps and pianos, whistles and drums and other odd instruments carved from petrified wood or sewn in the strangest of cloths. I was enthralled. The commander had banned music on his ships, although that was the least of his cruelties. Nico knew from the moment she saw me, trailing behind him, how he treated me. How he treated us all. And she offered to bargain for me." I stop myself, struck by the feeling that, instead of bringing me closer to Nico, the stranger's story will pull her further away from me than ever.

But he presses on. "Nico knew about the map too. And as the commander walked in here, it called out to her, running along her scars and trying to find its way to her. No matter, mapmaker, that you had tattooed it in black and violet and umber on his skin, it sought her out. I'm right in thinking that you could never recreate it from memory?"

I shake my head, reliving the night the commander blindfolded me, placed the tattoo implements in my hand, and brought his prisoners in one by one, to describe those lands and seas and journeys to me. I had just been a conduit for the directions of their words, then witness to the sounds of their subsequent executions. One by one by one.

"Some maps are not mine to know. The ink mixed with his blood and that brought it under his rule..." I stop as the stranger brings his finger to his lips to silence me. The rhythmic footfalls of the soldiers pound towards us, stop outside my shop. I hold my breath – has someone found me out, or is it the stranger they are looking for? He whispers something in an unfamiliar tongue. The gas lamps flicker, someone shouts from the direction of the public house, and the soldiers run from my door.

"For nearly a year, you and Nico shared the shop. You selling your diagrams of dreams and places unknowable, she balladlining for the sad and the lost, the greedy and the curious. Almost a year, until the night the commander returned again, demanding to know why the song he had bought didn't control the map, why instead his crew had all died or gone mad crossing the Bitter Seas. Why it called lamiae who attached themselves to the hull of his ship and sucked the life from it so it ended up a wraith-vessel, unable to make it back to shore. But Nico gazed very calmly at him and said—"

"Some maps are not yours to know," I finish. In the low light, the foxes curl up and tuck their noses into their tails and the animal bones huddle close to autumn leaf capes. The parchment sways and bounces on the wall, blown by a fierce breeze from its far reaches.

"The commander's blade was quicker than either of you thought possible. But Nico's arm caught the first blow and a harpy shriek bled from the wound. It brought him to his knees and you brained him with a ceramic urn. She bound her cut and directed you to strip his shirt and stake him out, face down. 'No blindfold this time, dear heart,' she told you. There was the map, scrimshawed by you across his back. You gathered your tools and sat at this very counter, and Nico took your sharpest-nibbed pen, opening the balladline that ran from her collarbone to navel."

With the stranger's words, it is as though she stands before me now, pale flesh crossed by a thousand scars, each one a path to exquisite music. A path that is paved in pain and one that she walked gladly again and again. It is as though I can hear the notes spilling from her torso. That song has anchored itself somewhere deep inside me too. I hold my breath, feeling faint, worrying that the soldiers will come back, that the stranger does not know the end of this tale, that I will be anchored to the past until the end of my days. That the stranger *does* know the end of it and that there will be another loss to add to the store of them I have already accumulated.

My guest draws a deep breath and closes his eyes. "The refrain that bled from that wound was like the light that flashes through opals made into sound. Like all the minor keys twined themselves into notes so discordantly, gloriously melancholic that they bade the ocean to stop tiding, the wind to stay in its own corner of the world, the blood in your veins to stop flowing, all to right an awful wrong. She sung the map from his skin through you and onto the parchment that hangs on that wall."

He opens his eyes and continues, as I cannot speak. "You drew the last landfall, then collapsed and watched as Nico, with quiet words and gentle hands, sealed the balladline once more. She knew you would not be able to assist her with what needed to be done next. So she put you to bed, whispered to keep the map safe until its owner came to claim it. When you woke the next morning, both she and the commander were gone and the map hung in that very spot."

The lamps brighten again, although the air has the ghost-scent of warm blood, as it had that night. The stranger looks at me sadly. I steady myself, so my voice won't waver.

"There was a great commotion the next morning, for the commander's body was found floating face-down in the fen, wrapped in weed and fish-nibbled at the toes. They said he had bled out from the lacerations on his back. But with no crew to seek vengeance and certainly no love lost between him and Rorkenbach's troops, they didn't bother to investigate further. Although the whispers about me continue. Still..." I shrug.

"And Nico?" he asks.

"I haven't seen her since that day. But she is still regarded as trouble here and would be executed on sight if she returned." In the years since she left, the weight of loss has lightened a little, but grief still feathers its way across my skin. Then the map shakes impatiently and I stand, lift it from the wall. I roll it carefully and seal it with bronze wax that only the one who knows its story will be able to break.

"I believe this belongs to you, sir." But I hesitate as I go to hand it over. Yes, he has told me the true story. But it is a story of the past and no hint of how I might leave here, where I might begin my search for Nico. I am bound by the lore of cartography, but for the first time I want to disobey it. I want something for *myself*.

As he puts his hand out his coat rises up his wrist a little, revealing a criss-crossing of old scars that remind me of hers. Tears well up in my eyes and I turn, lay the map out of his reach, and busy myself with the tea urn so he will not see. "But of what use is the map to you without the song that he took from Nico?"

Behind me, he laughs softly, then, in a very familiar voice, says, "I only used it once, dear heart. That song and the map are mine alone to know."

I want to move, but that voice, those words, have frozen me to the spot.

"Thank you for keeping it safe. I cannot stay, but we will meet again. You have my word. You have this, for yourself. No one else."

I turn, and with the sharp beak of the magpie skull on the counter, Nico, in the guise of pirate and raconteur, opens up a balladline on her palm. The place where she keeps her secret songs. Then the music…it whispers into my ears and finds its way into the places where I keep my own secrets. It moves through me stealthy and sure, like flame, like water, like the soft creep of a bee deciding where it will sting. Her song, clear and ancient and raw, fills me with memories gone and those to come.

It banishes the terrible emptiness that has lived in me forever.

It is Nico's gift and it sets me free.

She seals the line with a whisper and it is Nico's lips that press softly to my cheek. I hand the map to her, my protector and the only friend I have ever known. Nico, shapeshifting Balladliner, who disappears again under her shadow-coat as I lift my hand to her cheek. On the counter is the silver skull ring, eyes shining from within. I slip it on my thumb as my artefact maps – those I know and love – shift and settle on the shelves, happy that the ghastly map, the last reminder of my other life, is gone for good.

As the song beats softly as a promise inside me, I set the flame a little higher under the samovar, then open the door to the night patrons who navigate their way to me under the unchartered depths of a dark and starry sky.

a nightingale's map of the city

The white stone buildings of the city gleam like scattered pearls, their peaks and towers reaching for the vertiginous blue of the sky. Atop the spires and turrets and minarets, domes and curlicues of gold-leaf sparkle, making the city seem dusted with slow-burning embers. The ghost of the giant Gustav, the city's architect and creator, walks cobbled alleyways that are carpeted in moss, skimming past the tiny ferns growing from arched doorways. It is the city he built for his flame-haired Julietta. His place of torment since the day she left.

Everywhere – *everywhere* – are monuments to Julietta. Ivy-covered statues, beaten copper friezes, emerald-roofed cenotaphs carved with elegiac verses. As though all of them together might be woven into a spell under the splinter-moon to bring her back again. Julietta left the city long ago, much longer than Gustav cares to remember. So he holds the city close like a well-worn photograph, folded and re-folded and disintegrating with time. Without it, he's scared that he wouldn't remember her face, her voice, the touch of her skin.

Sometimes, he thinks he sees her as a silver shadow slipping through the streets, leaving an unearthly sheen on the darkening stone. In spring, he glimpses her running in her yellow velvet cape towards the opera house, flanked by the singing fae who bear the remnants of her voice.

Gustav tries to be content with the scraps time has left behind. But doubt frays his edges. Once, this was a city for two. But before she left, Julietta opened the city to mortals, left it behind for them like a discarded toy. He can't remember if, in doing so, she had been deliberately cruel or just thoughtless. The people now living there are tiny and insignificant and shiver just a little when they pass through Gustav's ghost as he sits by the glass butterfly house or, in petulant moments, sprawls across the palace steps.

In the city of giants, of grandeur and vast sorrow, jewels and alabaster, red-haired sylphs float, unseen by its inhabitants, who are busy in the business of being ordinary. They are wisps of women, a thousand images of Julietta woven and rewoven, painted and sung, sculpted and remembered and reshaped in the years since she left.

Red-haired sylphs float as twists of breeze or phrases of song the ear can't quite catch. They drift and glide, wrapped in tresses studded with tiny blue flowers, smiling lasciviously at Gustav, who can only watch as people overrun his city.

He stares at the sky. He wonders, yet again, if one day the sylphs will forget him too.

They wrap themselves around him and whisper:

We are echoes too.

Gustav shakes them free. He does not feel like listening to them today, whispering in her voice about the roads she might have taken, the places she might be found. Reminding him that he no longer remembers exactly the colour of her eyes, or whether she smelled of rosewater or sandalwood. As though unfolding the old photograph, he traces his hands over the lines of the buildings and the streets, where each day the gold dulls a little, the cobbles wear just a bit more. Only the ghosts of giants and half-maidens who were never more than an imitation remember how it felt when the city had its soul. The warm pliability of compliant stone; the seasons that formed themselves around Julietta's moods.

The door to the palace, banded with iron curled into daemons and lovers and winged serpents that change with the light, resists his touch. Beyond are frescoed rooms, gas lamps, and clockwork faeries to serve a princess's every need. But the door stands firm, the treasures beyond it shielded from sight.

The longer she is gone, the more your city slips away from you. Only the doors with gilded handles are open to you now, the sylphs sigh. Gustav can count those handles on one hand. They fade further every day. He sits heavily on the marble outside the butterfly house – to the mortals it feels like a squall of wind gusting by – and presses his ghostly nose to the glass. Butterflies – sapphire, citrine, fuchsia, amber – flit up to him as though he is a honeyed treat laid out by their keepers. Above the entrance, a clockwork butterfly, an imitation of the real ones inside, flutters its wings, takes flight on the quarter hour then lands again. The sylphs stroke Gustav's hands, trying to cheer him in their sweetly savage way.

Once upon a time, an emperor's courtiers built a nightingale from glass and rubies and gold and ribbons. The emperor loved the clockwork bird much more than he had ever loved the real one, with her plain brown feathers and unpredictable tune. Yet she continued to love him long after he had forgotten her in favour of the imitator.

The giant poked his finger moodily at the glass, scattering the butterflies.

Your Julietta, she waited for you as long as she could, dearest, while you were building her memorials. She had cities inside her, waiting for you. Vast and unpredictable and waiting to be explored. One day, all the doors here will be closed to you and you will just be thunder fading in the distance. That is the way of echoes, dear Gustav.

If they weren't so like her, he would wrap their flaming tresses around their throats. Swallows dart and swoop from the sky, skimming through his chest in a gust of air. He follows them as they make their way back to their nests in the city's walls, which were carved with stories written for Julietta, lit at different hours by the sun or moon. The swallows have burrowed through the words so the stories are now just nonsense phrases.

…creature of star-flecked night, chasing
a hollow moon and ever-ebbing tides…

…she reaches for the belly of winter, pushing against diaphanous clouds…

…silver and green, its rhythm mirroring the ocean crashing through her, speaking to the moon moths and wind-ridden gulls…

Is there nothing left in the city that remains as it was in the beginning?

Gustav walks along the wall, reading its broken stories in the late afternoon light. He stops at the southwest corner, where he had long ago tethered a hot air balloon to the wall with creeping vines of purple roses and ruby-seeded pomegranates. He used to bring Julietta here, lift her up to sit in the basket to view the city, its architecture his ever-expanding love letter to her. Surely she had never doubted his heart, laid bare in the streets and passageways and grand buildings with their solid language of stone? But it is this corner to which she made her own way one day, climbing the tethers and scattering purple blooms and red, red seeds in her wake. It is the corner from which she made her escape.

The word jolts Gustav and he repeats it aloud, rolls it around on his tongue. "Escape. Escape..." Until today, he had always thought of her as running away, having left him and spurned his gift of her own city. But that word – *escape* – bubbled up from a forgotten city deep inside him.

Another broken story on the wall glows golden in the afternoon light; like the gilded handles, it admits him to somewhere that could easily have been lost.

...true, you are skin-hungry, your desire washed to
a faded wraith-story of missing her.
But it was not she who doubted...

With that quiet realisation, Gustav sees his city as Julietta must have seen it, in the end.

"My dearest Julietta, there is nothing of you here," he whispers to the swallows as they dive through the air. The rose vine is just thorns now, tangled among the pomegranates that have run wild. As he speaks, one of the wispy wraiths, a distant echo of Julietta whose colour has faded to a rosy silver, snakes through the vine. She beckons to him, giggling, and curls herself at the base of one of the rose bushes.

He pushes his hands through the vines towards her. She fades until nothing is left but a beating light the colour of the sun. Reaching further, towards the buttery glow, Gustav wishes that he could feel the thorns scratching at his skin. Chunks from the wall are scattered among the gnarled roots of the bush, the carved words insensible as even sentences, let alone stories.

Curlew. Spice. Glimmer-deep. Longing.

Two of those clay-cast words glow in the aftermath of the sylph's touch, a lighthouse call across the years to Gustav.

Find me.

They gleam brighter as he stares at them. ***Find me.***

He thinks about all the things that she loved: moonlight, early morning, stone bridges over fast-flowing rivers. He smiles as the memories rush through him pulse-quick. Bitter chocolate, wild storms, autumn frost, the light of deepest winter.

He stares at the sky. He wonders. Then he begins to run, along the wall, through the gates, up and down the streets until he finds the sylphs giggling and splashing in the city's central fountain.

What happened to the emperor? Gustav asks.

The clockwork bird ran down and the real nightingale came back, singing him songs from the cherry tree, singing him back from death.

The sun sets, the changeling light serpentine as it twists through hidden alleys and doorways collapsing on themselves. Gustav lies on the cold earth as the sylphs pull the darkness over themselves like a blanket. Sighing, crooning, slipping into sleep.

This city is a story no one bothers to read, a clockwork nightingale whose gears have rusted silent. But as Gustav lies down next to his red-haired sylphs who smell of cinnamon and autumn, he no longer sees Julietta's pale flesh in the alabaster stone. Julietta's smile peeking from the ivy statues. Julietta's touch in the mist that rolls from the palace windows.

He stares at the indigo sky. He knows what he must do.

Tomorrow, the city may fade a little more, but it no longer matters, for he will not be here to witness it. Tomorrow, he will leave from the corner of roses and pomegranates, and follow the winds that took her away. With those two burning bright words – ***find me*** – he will search across land and ocean, seasons and storms.

He will find her and they will build a new city together, one of bridges and clock towers without hands to stop the passage of time. A city not of stone, but of all the thoughts and longings unspoken that fill the spaces between the rooftops and hover above the streets. With sylphs and olive-plump moons and infinite brightness inked by their careful hands. A city that they will call home, with unchartered streets they will explore together. Be she old and faded, or bones and ghost, Julietta will write her own words on the walls and Gustav will beg her leave to map the cities running wild inside her.

at the still point

Alice and her wild song. That's why I'm here, wandering the shore from dawn until dusk, collecting bottled messages the current drags in. Sometimes, I think I hear the hoarse whistle of a steam train, heading for the main station that sings its own tune in the voice of a thousand travellers.

Then I remember there's nothing between the shore and the city for five hundred miles, except the rust farm that stretches further than anyone can map. The owner, a withered old man who looks and smells like autumn, is kind enough, but he can afford to be. He's not looking for a way to put the broken pieces back together again.

Wild, in her Alice-song. It was the music that found Alice, not the other way around. The voices she sung in, you could lose yourself to them. One was too many and a thousand were never enough. It was fire and fury and fierceness unbound. She sung to me the things I never knew were missing. Alice, wildly unravelling me from myself.

Wild Alice and her carnival of songs. Why don't I hear those in the wind instead of steam-train ghosts and the too-steady shush of the waves? I long for the cat's footstep plink of plucked violins, the arrhythmic drums, the mournful sax that were her music. She used to sing throughout the night and into the next day. When she finished, I watched her undress, sweat sheening her skin like oil. Then she would undress me and whisper quiet ballads across my ribs, down the length of my spine, winding them around my bones. I may as well have shed my skin, the way she could find me despite myself.

Lost, in the wilderness of Alice.

* * *

We met on the last night of the carnival, when the popcorn was stale and the grounds trampled to a muddy slush. It was said the Leader liked the idea of travelling carnivals, that it was good for the people. Secretly, they reminded me of better times. Tinny harmonies made of an off-beat four/four time, an old accordion and a mandolin hanging in the air with cheap cigar smoke and the grassy smell of show horses. The music was a pale green and yellow, bursting and fading before me as I walked. Not everyone sees it the way I do, although I was nine years old before I realized that music is plain for most people.

I wandered the carnival for hours, not wanting to return to my empty apartment. Slowly, the shouts from the carousel and the upside down pirate ship thinned, and the crowd became a group of stragglers under the buzzing strings of lights (a kind of constant burnt-orange that hurt my eyes).

The ocean wind picked up as the lights shut down, one by one. I closed my eyes as the salt air blew away the mustiness of the carnival. A far away singing made my stomach drop. That tiny wisp of melody, carried on the wind, was bright azure, lasting long after the notes stopped. While the carnies were packing up and the last few patrons were being herded toward the exits, I slipped between the tents, in the direction of her voice, a streak of teal against the shadowed night.

At the edge of the carnival, where the cliff dropped away to the sea, was a smaller tent that would only fit, perhaps, thirty people. It was empty, but a slip of a woman in a plain black dress stood on the edge of the cliff, letting the cold air gooseflesh her bare arms. She turned and smiled at me.

"You're too late for the show, I'm afraid."

I nodded. "I heard you singing and…this being the last night and all, I…" I suddenly felt foolish, standing there in the dark.

"It's okay, you didn't miss much anyway. The front row was filled with some rather grim men who didn't really seem to enjoy it. Brought the whole mood down."

I just nodded as she looked out across the ocean, toward the headland where the lighthouse shone its staccato beam toward the horizon.

"But since it is the last night…" She turned and disappeared inside the little tent. A moment later, the crackle of a phonograph then a three am blues piano lick, sad and arrow-hearted. Azure tinged with violet, a soft aurora dancing along the cliff's edge.

Then Alice began to sing, a fork of lightning-gold against firework bursts of creamy pearl, fading then crackling into life again as she crested and troughed each phrase. Until then, the world had been monochrome.

In that untamed moment, Alice gave me music and colours that I never imagined were possible. She gave me that to remember, to the grave and beyond. There's only ever been Alice from that moment on.

* * *

The next morning was dull and blustery as I caught the tram to work. Down Main Street lined with fancy glass doors leading to the most expensive apartments in the town, through the gothic quarter where the paint was peeling and squatters peered down from graffiti-scarred windows, along the sea front where the wind whipped foam from atop the breakers onto the tram windows. Atop the cliff, the carnival tents and streamers flapped forlornly in the dull morning, looking no closer to breaking down and moving.

The agents were waiting for me when I arrived at work, three of them in dark clothes with darker smiles. I'd never seen them before, but they made me uneasy.

"We'd like to second you for a top-level project." The woman in the middle spoke first. It clearly wasn't an offer, but an order. "It's in relation to the use of auditory area fields in combat."

They'd lost me before they'd even begun. "I'm just an administrator though."

"Your synaesthesia is of particular interest to us in research that we're currently undertaking."

The three of them began speaking rapid fire about concepts and a project I hadn't even known existed until then.

Sonic weaponry.

Ultrasound to damage ears, to vibrate eyeballs and produce vague, wraith-like apparitions.

Vibro-acoustic stimulation to reset the rhythm of a heart or to stop it all together.

Sound to induce hallucinations and targeted tissue-shearing.

"Sound as a weapon?" I heard myself say. They stopped abruptly and the first woman pinned me with her hard gaze.

"To date, yes. But that's where you come in. Not just sound as a weapon. Music."

* * *

I walked for a while after they'd briefed then dismissed me, wandered back through the gothic quarter, almost hoping that someone might pull me into the shadows of an old, crumbling mansion, or injure me badly enough that I wouldn't have to go through with the project. They're not trying to be cruel, I told myself, they're just carrying out orders.

I felt gutted, emptied, all the same. Could they not just leave one thing for me to keep for myself? Never before had I wished that my world could be just like everyone else's. If it was, then they wouldn't be asking me to help them understand how to use music to injure and kill people. If that was my world, then I could have listened to a woman called Alice sing for me in the small hours of the night, then let that memory evaporate as the years ticked by.

I found myself on the foreshore. The carnival's Ferris wheel was moving slowly. Someone was repainting its weathered sign. *Do they know why they have to stay?* I wondered.

* * *

Had it not been for the death of the Poet, Alice may have gone unnoticed. The Poet died the day after the Leader was voted into power, years earlier. It was the last popular vote we will ever likely see, since elections have now been dispensed with.

It was said that the Poet took to his bed upon hearing the election results, his windows open to the rain and violent winds that stormed their own symphony along the shore. It was said that he sung his last refrain and the wind carried it through the streets, into the poorest corners and the homes of the despairing. It lit those who needed light and wrapped its dark fingers around the throats of those who sought to spread their own hateful darkness. Not enough to kill, only to disturb and unsettle. Enough to say *Our time will come again.*

It was whispered that as the wind died, so too did the Poet, at the still point after the storm. His songs were still sung and danced, and thrilled through us in later years, but not being sung in his voice they were useless for the project. So the agents told me that morning.

So long after the death of the Poet, they'd found another whose voice could serve them. They needed Alice, they told me, and would be using me to capture her tune. To turn it into a weapon to defend their hateful rule.

I had only the rainbow fire that the music of others gave me. And they would use it against me. For unless I wanted to disappear and be wiped from memory, I would have to find Alice again and take apart her song.

* * *

A caged bird never sings as candid and joyful and true as one that is free.

I think that was why they didn't just take her. Nothing is as powerful, as potent, as that which is freely given. I knew that through my own slide into the moral grey. It isn't a quick descent, a lightning leap from who you are to the thing that you hate. You justify the first slips, just move the bar a little each time, until you're trapped in an endlessly repeating dirge.

Night after night I went to listen to Alice. She left a tracery of scales and chords across my skin, made me sheen like some creature dug up from the night. *Sing me up and sing me down.* Each night was its own winding path through a secret city I never knew existed.

I had a reserved seat, to the left of the door to her tent. Alice sang in the round, accompanied by the old brass phonograph that crackled and sighed as though it loved her. The night always began with songs in major keys, G and F, sometimes B if she was feeling playful. Those keys were bright and glittering, dragonfly chants hovering in the air before us. Through their wings we saw the stars.

As time ticked on toward the small hours, the songs became sadder, minor keys, velvet-rich loam hues of indigo and midnight and cinnabar. The audience would hold their breath and sometimes cry. Alice was their escape. Her performance was different every night, except for the last number. A Lydian oeuvre that was shadowed yet bright, limned in silver. It split her own shadow into crescent slivers dancing and scything their way through the audience. The slivers sashayed and paused behind audience members most visibly affected by Alice's voice, bending over them like animals sniffing prey. It made me think of the Poet's final song, twining its way around the throats of the unsuspecting, and I knew, then, exactly what they wanted me to take from her.

I hated myself for knowing that.

Night after night, I hoped it would be different. But it was always the inevitable ending.

On the fifth night – the fifth always has a way of bringing us back to the beginning – the small audience emptied out after the show, and it was just me and Alice and the waves breaking far below the cliffs.

"So, you're it then?" She *almost* sounded amused.

I nodded. What point was there in denying it? The regime's reach was all-encompassing and we had all known enough disappeared people to know that there's no outrunning the Leader's agents. And I worked for them.

"How did you know?"

"They haven't stopped us from leaving just because they like the show." Alice smiled and touched my face, bee-soft. "Besides, you're the only one who comes in here, night after night, and who leaves looking scared."

* * *

Sing me something red, something crimson and brutal.

B-flat minor, verse/chorus/verse/crescendo/chorus/end. Each note a different tinct, but all against that red, red palette. Like a spray of blood.

Sing me something violet, the blooms of widows' tears.

F-sharp major, a soprano trill through the blue tones, lifting me on saltwater wings.

Sing me up, sing me down, sing me through the night and round
The colours of your naked heart, that beats
the blood of song.

Alice and her wild heart. She knew what I was to do, and she let herself love me anyway.

Sang herself across my skin and I, in my clumsy, fragile way, sharpened her edges and brightened her flesh until she shone in a fragmented riot like a church window at first light.

"Is every sound a colour for you?" She ran her finger across my damp collarbone.

"Only music and sounds that have a musical tone." I turned to face her, imagining that she kept that wonderful voice locked away somewhere inside, letting it out like a pet cat to play in the night.

"Tell me what it's like," she murmured.

How do you tell someone what it's like to be you? "There are shades that I've never seen in life that I see when you sing. It's not just the notes or the keys, it's the way it's put together...the timbre, the drum beat, the role of each instrument. Your voice."

I turned my back on her, swung my legs over the edge of the bed, unable to bear the touch of her hand on my traitor's skin. "How can you stand me, knowing what it is they want me to do? To tear apart your music, to use it as a *weapon*? I can barely stand myself, for God's sake!"

She wrapped her thin arm around my waist, dropped kisses the length of my spine as she sat up, then rested her chin on my shoulder. "Then don't do it."

"You know that's not an option."

"No, I know it's the difficult option, but ultimately, isn't it your choice?"

I laughed, bitter-green. "Not if I want to wake up tomorrow. Even if I didn't already work for them, if they came to me with this, how could I possibly say no?"

She stood then, wrapped in the sheet, and looked down at me. "If we had a way of saying no, without them even knowing it, would you do it?"

I shivered. That was sedition, a word I didn't want to think of, let alone say aloud. Alice and her wild ways.

"Would you?" she asked again, no longer looking like my midnight chanteuse but like a fighter.

I shook my head and, in a coda of silence, dressed and left behind my Alice.

***

I walked through the streets, angry at myself and at her. How could she ask me to refuse? It terrified me. But to use her in the way they wanted was crueller than just wanting to develop an ordinary weapon. It was taking something sacred and destroying it. It was the immortality of her songs that they wanted. Immortal music to become immortal weapons, to be used over and over again. A siren call to gather people at the still point, and then tear them apart.

Did Alice really think it was so easy for me to back away from that? I had already lodged my first report, given them a sample to use in their testing, told them about the midnight music and how people reacted to it. They were excited about moving the project ahead.

"And she affects them in the same way that *he* did?" The grey, grim woman wouldn't mention the Poet by name, just like the rest of them. I nodded, dutiful by habit.

"But I will need more time to learn how to harness it. It is a delicate business, after all, and I want to be sure I get the very best from her." Dutiful by fear, as well.

It began to rain, bringing me back to my pointless marching through the deserted streets. Even though I'd twisted and turned through dark alleys and down bright, gaslit main roads, I realized I was heading back towards her.

Didn't she know that, even if I could somehow say no, they'd send another in my place? They had lost the Poet and they wouldn't simply let Alice go, even if I failed. And if not me, then who?

I had lived in the city all my life and had never met anyone who saw and felt music in the same way that I did. So anyone else who they used for the project would likely be someone with knowledge, but not my peculiar expertise. They would likely be brutal in using Alice's song and breaking it apart for their weapons. Perhaps break Alice in the process.

I left the cobbled streets, slowly walking up the unpaved path to the carnival. Back to her van, to try to explain to her that there was no way other than this. Soft, yellow light shone from the windows, peeking around the edges of the curtains. The sound of urgent muttering inside stopped me. The door opened. Two women and a man each kissed Alice on both cheeks, then melted away into the shadows.

I stepped forward, but she stopped me with a railway signal glare, her eyes a red light.

In an instant, it became clear why she let herself love me, even though she knew what I had to do. Alice had secrets of her own, which three people slinking into the early hours revealed more clearly than our hours alone ever could have.

The world turned to black and white.

Alice was Resistance.

* * *

Resistance was secret messages encoded in the graffiti that covered the buildings in the gothic quarter. It was dangerous and deadly and barely visible. It was meetings of two or three or five in the old brick cellars of bars, which were rumoured to stretch out in tunnels under the city. It was code in lyrics, a way to pass on instructions and words of hope. Words of a secret war, waged in the shadows.

Alice had kept her secret well. Between the two of us, she was the dangerous one.

You gathered the words in your cheeks
Saved them for winter, as though I'm an ice-skin on water
Waiting for you, to fall through
A murder of darkness
A crow-fall of sadness

"This is what you meant then, by refusing without them knowing."

She held the door open for me, not running from a confrontation – not like me – and we stood in that small, yellow-lit space, trying to make sense of what might happen next.

The still point, fraught with possibility.

"You can carry out your work, report back, play the good worker, but ultimately, what you take will be used by us, instead, to create weapons for our side. We can keep you safe."

"How do you know I won't turn you in?"

Alice smiled, reached across to touch my hand. "Because you're not one of them. Not really."

Be the warm spring that breaks me,
The voice that breaks the crow-fall
The smile to my call

I imagined crowds gathering, the music entrancing them, then the screaming as their muscles tore from their bones, organs shut down, bleeding from their eyes and ears. Then, the awful silence. I wanted to tell her that I didn't have a choice, but it wasn't true. That was the moment I made my choice. I squeezed her hand and moved from the stillness into the luminous music again.

* * *

The empty cavern of an abandoned church, dusty parquetry floor under dustier light flooding in from the eastern window. An intricate, dirty stained-glass window of forgotten saints. An open-lidded grand piano, keys yellow with disuse.

Alice walked, barefoot, to the piano, ran her fingers across the keys in a chromatic scale of popping bulbs of colour. The notes inhabited the space, as though the deserted church was a vast echo chamber in which the music could endlessly ricochet.

They had given me everything I needed. Bottles for echo chambers, to capture the resonances of sound. An abandoned church in which to work. But only finite time. They were growing impatient.

Emptying my bag, I held bottle after bottle to the wire of each note as Alice played, slower this time, the glass reverberating with the resonance of each note. While they still vibrated, I set each bottle in rainbow order, identifiable after the notes dimmed.

Alice began to sing and we gently shattered her song apart, into puzzle pieces that only I would be able to identify. I carved them apart, asking for a repetition of this word, or that key change. Then I coaxed the shapes – mandalas and birds and amorphous shadows – into the glass bottles and vials, matching the phrase or bass line or single notes held just so, into the little resonance chamber that complemented and underscored it. Empty, they had vibrated in my hands; filled with notes, phrases, canticles, they pulsed and shivered, electrified, in a constant dance tiding from side to side.

The still points I left until last. The still points are colourless and refract all music through them like a prism, splitting them into their own hues. The pauses, rests, the almost-silent intervals. In those still points were crammed the words that the songs could not contain. At the still point there is the silence of anticipation. I collected them in a little black bottle, stoppered it with a golden cork.

I looked at Alice, hands resting gently on the keys, staring out the window. I wondered what she thought, but I was too afraid to ask. Sometimes words threaten to shatter more than just the quiet moments, and I couldn't bear to think that she might not love me. That we might part and she would become just a mythologized memory of a person. As though she had never quite existed at all.

* * *

A hurried parting; Alice rushing to her show, me with our bottled treasure due to meet with her Resistance friends.

Only I turned left, instead of right, jumped on the tram that would take me to the Rip, the roughest part of the coast where two currents met and swirled, crashing on the rocks. I was the last passenger on the car. This was not a place frequented at night.

"Are you alright, brother?" the driver asked as I alighted, worry lining his face. It was, after all, a well-documented suicide spot.

I smiled and nodded. "Thanks. You'll be picking me up on the way back."

The ocean chorus was chartreuse, deep, and soothing in its ferocity. The water eddied at the meeting point of the currents, creating an undertow. Anything caught in it was pulled under and carried far out to sea.

Alice was right. I did have a choice. It just wasn't the choice she thought I would make. I unbuckled the bottles from the black bag and dropped them, one by one by one, into the Rip. I stood on the rocks and sent pieces of Alice and me out into the world. Messages in bottles, that someone, somewhere might find, uncork, and understand. I would not be a part of turning Alice's song into weapons, into things to destroy and maim and kill. I would not let the music disappear like so many people had disappeared, a flash in time then gone, a palette of memory fading to nothing.

And perhaps somewhere, those tiny pieces of Alice and me would be the start of new songs and stories. Would be brought to life again.

The sea carried them away and washed me clean, as the gaslight of the return tram shone across the waves. I turned and walked towards it, putting my hand in my pocket to rest on the last, tiny bottle there.

The still points I would keep for myself.

* * *

On the tram home, I hummed softly to myself. I was out of tune, but it made me happy anyway. Two stops in, a man with a face as crinkled and brown as an autumn leaf walked slowly on and sat down beside me. I fell silent.

"I've studied the ocean currents in these parts for years, you know. I'm something of an amateur oceanographer. Salt air does the strangest thing to metals, you know. Anyway, those currents…" He smiled at me.

A trickle of sweat ran down my neck. The tram rattled on.

"So, what now?" he asked.

"I-I'm not sure I know what you mean…"

He pulled out a cigarette and lit it, as we wound our way down the hill, towards the city proper. "Well, you can't go back, is what I mean." His face became grave and he put his free hand over mine. On his wrist, a blurred tattoo of a bass clef – a signal of the old Resistance that had arisen at the same time the Leader came to power. "They came and took her tonight, in the middle of her show," he said softly. "I'm sorry."

* * *

Alice and her wild song. That's why I'm here, wandering the shore from dawn until dusk, collecting bottled messages the current drags in. The Resistance, they weren't happy when they found out what I'd done, but, strangely, they understood. Some of them had loved her too. I could barely stand after the rust farmer told me she'd gone, but he pulled me off the tram, held me up, and we escaped through the tunnels like rats.

I'm safe here, far from the city. And we're working on other ways to fight the regime, ways that are cunning and deadly. No word has reached us, yet, of song-weapons. No word, yet, of Alice, but we keep searching, the Resistance in its way and me in mine.

Two bottles so far have washed up here, home to an emerald coda and a tangerine, star-speckled snippet of soprano notes. Wild Alice and her life of contrasts. Sometimes, I expect her to wash in here like a siren, full of her wry smiles and a lullaby of forgiveness. Washing me away from myself.

The sea hasn't brought me anything today, only driftwood and a lazy silver chorale of spring tides. Before I head home, I sit on the sand, cooling quickly as the sun slides like butter below the horizon. I keep the jar full of still points with me always, a reminder that in silence, there is possibility. Putting the vessel to my ear, I open the stopper just a crack and the still points loop, over and over. They produce the sensation of skin on skin, as though she is sitting behind me, her lips pressed softly to my neck, her hand resting on mine.

She still finds me despite myself.

Lost, in the wilderness of Alice.

blackhearts and sorrowsong

Had the gargoyle, Mara, not carefully removed His Eminence's tongue and sewn his lips shut before the crucifixion, he would have screamed fit to bring the whole cathedral down. That was the thing about cruel men; their tolerance for their own suffering was shamefully low.

The crypt brimmed with darkness, thick and sour, except for the weak circle of yellow light from the candles Mara had lit. She had no need of the light, the eyesight of gargoyles being just as good in the darkness as day, but she wanted him to see her as she picked up each nail. As she walked softly toward him, mallet in hand. As she hammered each heavy spike through his flesh, sinew, bone and into the heavy wooden cross.

From the cathedral above, the voices of the choir were a comfort as she went about her work. Familiar as family, precise, unbound. As beautiful as solitude, or the tranquil dawn.

She drove the last of the nails into his feet, dropped the mallet, and bent to pick up the pale-covered book from the floor. It was the only thing that she would take with her; the only thing she could not leave behind. The Book had been her companion for almost ten years. She had found it in an abandoned casket in the reliquary, a tattered, unloved thing. Rescued it, she liked to think, mended it and gave it a new binding. *We are two broken halves make a whole,* the Book had told her when she sewed the final stich. Now, it felt as though it was a slumbering creature in her arms.

Mara leaned in to the Cardinal, her clawed hand gentle on his shoulder.

"There was a time I wanted to love you, you know," she said.

His head had already dropped to his chest and she doubted whether he had heard her at all.

* * *

Mara stopped running and crouched under the bridge, the sorrowsong of the choir skimming across the river. It wouldn't be long before they found the Cardinal's body and began looking for her. His Eminence's *petit daemon*. They would expect her to leap across the rooftops, flying like a bat under the crescent moon. Not to scurry through the streets like a common rat.

The taste of starlight was sharp on her tongue as she gulped the night air. It reminded her of her life, centuries before, when she and her clan had run across the city roofs on the nights the ghouls had threatened war and the wolves had been bold enough to invade her city. When the gargoyles had scampered up and down its walls under brisk winter skies, leaping after the invaders and carrying them to the top of the tower, to drop them in the fires below. The city had been reborn beneath them and the gargoyles were heroes. Protectors of the city. Those were the times before her kin had been trapped within stone and she was cursed to be the only one of her kind to still draw breath.

The priests of the new church – the ones who wanted to defeat Death herself – had made clear the way of their god. There was no room for creatures that looked like animals, but spoke and loved like humans.

"We will keep just one," His Eminence at the time had said, "for the purposes of posterity."

She had been handed down as a pet from priest to priest for nigh on eight decades.

Mara raised her left hand to her throat, clutching the Book tightly in her right. The shadow memory of the iron collar they had forced her to wear made her feel as though she were on the verge of choking. The sorrowsong grew louder, voices weaving into an invisible chain pulling her back toward the cathedral. How could it be a place that she reviled, and also a place that, at times, had lifted her beyond the heights any gargoyle had reached with their wings. Surely the delicate chain of voices could not be stronger than the chain the Cardinal had kept her on, clipped to the iron collar. The same chain with which she had bound him to the cross, before pinning him to it, outstretched like the butterflies he used to study. In the gloaming candlelight, she had imagined an outline of wings protruding from his shoulder blades, a ghost of hollow bone and angel-membrane in the dark.

She hugged the Book to her chest, shook the memory away as the choir ceased its singing. In its wake, the night was soundless but for the scrabbling of rats in the gardens and the splash of an oar nearby. Then a thin scream unspooled across the water. Mara's breath quickened.

The crucifixion was a secret no longer.

Church bells tolled across the night and it was too late to run, too late to take to the skies. *Hide!* Instinct took over. Gripping the Book tightly in her right hand, she hooked a talon through the lacework of the iron girder of the bridge and climbed upward, hanging upside down from her hands and feet and hoping it would be enough.

Below her, a pair of oars pulled through the water, stopping as the unseen boat thunked against the river bank. Mara curled herself tighter. Shifting to get a better grip, the Book squirmed in her hand and tumbled into the wooden raft below.

She let go of the bridge, turning to land, cat-like, in the boat and scooped up the Book, baring her teeth at the hooded figure holding the oars at the other end.

He raised his hands, showing he was unarmed. "My name is Jareth. We want the same thing," he whispered. "We've not much time. I'll get us away from here."

The boat slipped through the shadows of the willows that lined the banks. Mara breathed deeply, trying to slow her fast-beating heart and wondering how she might escape, if needs must.

"Where are you taking me?" Mara asked. She hadn't thought so far ahead as to what would happen *after*. After she had killed His Eminence. After she had escaped. Mara had been enslaved for so long, she wasn't sure that there ever could be anything *after*.

"*His Eminence*," Jareth spat out the title, "is a Blackheart."

"I know," Mara replied. "Though you must mean *was* a Blackheart, not *is*. He's nothing more now than a corpse hanging from a wooden cross."

"Is he?" Jareth pointed to the cathedral as they glided past it.

In the moonlight, a creature as slick and dark as oil shivered its way up its walls. One moment, a cockroach skitter, the next a mellifluous dance around the leaded windows and the grotesques lining the eaves. It leapt to the top of the belltower and stood taller than any man or creature should, spreading its wings to block out the stars. A ghost of hollow bone and angel-membrane in the dark.

* * *

Hundreds of years before, when Mara had been very young and her clan was revered within the city, there had been no Blackhearts. It was a time when men and women fell in love with gargoyles. The gargoyles took them into their secret roof cities, teaching them the knowledge of other worlds, worshipping the goddess of night and Sister Death. The women wore chains of jet in the hair, the men sapphires on their hands. The gargoyles tipped their wings with the same gems, wearing their betrothal for all to see. Then there were the children. The Garem, they called them…

"Keep your hands inside the boat," Jareth said, interrupting Mara's reverie.

Mara pulled her hands back, just as a diaphanous limb snaked its way towards her. She peered into the water; wraiths swam just beneath the surface, creating the currents with their smooth, nebulous limbs. Tiny bulbs of light fizzed and popped around their ever-changing forms, and within them, pulsing like heartbeats. As they flared, they lit the outline of pale golden cauls covering the backs of those souls, achingly bright against the ghost-dark. Mara gasped. Not just ordinary spirits, then. Ghosts of the vanished children of gargoyles and humans.

"This is a corpse road?" she asked.

Jareth nodded as he pulled his oars inside the craft as it sped, faster, faster, against the river's natural current. "The Blackheart will be heading to *L'Empire De La Mort*. We need to stop him before he gets there."

Mara hugged the Book to her chest, tracing the outline of the tattooed heart imprinted on the cover. Once she had made it whole again, it had whispered to her the spell that would bring about the end of the

Blackhearts, and set the world to rights. Something, though, had gone wrong in the execution. The dreadful Blackheart silhouette against the sky told her that. Riffling through the Book, with its ink sketches, illuminated letters, calligraphed spells, she came to that spell, and ran her finger down the centre of the two pages. The sharp edge of cut paper was a shock under her fingertip. She looked closer.

The next three pages had been removed.

His Eminence had played her for the fool that she was.

Her hand hovered over the paper edge, where the sheets of paper had been cut away. She closed her eyes, sure that, just for a moment, she could feel their ghosts drifting underneath her fingertips.

Shaking the past off, Mara looked ahead, to where yew trees replaced the willows and the river curved out of sight. Mausoleums in lichen skin guarded the bank: granite weeping women, their gowns eroded by time and grief, stood sentry under the moonlight. They were not headed for the tiny wharf that stood ready to receive the coffins that came to the cemetery by water. Instead, the corpselights below them bobbed and looped and pushed them toward a cleft in the bank.

Silent as the grave, they slipped through the opening, into the Undercity.

* * *

Undercity. A place of chimeras, who had crept upwards from their deep sleep beneath the earth, and the beggars and vagabonds from above. Unwanted and errant creatures from all realms passed through here, where tame wolves roamed the alleyways and stood guard in the catacombs lined with aging brown bones. As the city above had grown, so too had Undercity. Layer over layer, on the remnants of the old. Discarded tunnels and ancient crypts from abandoned churches. Life sprung from death.

Lanterns hung from the ceiling and shone from alcoves, lighting the way for monsters and humans alike. Tonight, though, the streets were strangely empty. A chimera's tail slithered around a corner and out of sight; firelight glowed in the windows of ramshackle homes, but there was no rattle of usual life. Undercity was holding its breath.

Waiting.

Mara, too, breathed shallowly. She gripped Jareth's arm.

"What is it?" he asked.

"I don't know. It seems as though with each step I feel more and more compelled to turn back. And I feel...I don't know...heavier, somehow."

Jareth pulled Mara gently into the lamplight, held her hand out to inspect it. He pressed his fingers to her hand and she could not feel his skin against hers; when he drew away, the flesh did not spring back.

"I'm getting too far from home," she whispered. "I don't want to die in here, turned to stone like my ancestors."

"I always believed that was a myth," he replied. "Perhaps then we could simply wait and try to stop him here..." Jareth sounded uncertain.

"Don't you have a plan?"

"I only knew that I needed to find you..."

"Why? How could you know—"

"You're the last gargoyle. And I am the last of the Garem."

The Garem – the otherworldly children of the gargoyles and humans. Cloaked in human skin, wings folded beneath golden cauls. They flew on feast nights, on the summer and winter solstices. They lived in the secret rooftop cities and wandered the streets of the city below at dawn and dusk, sweeping away sin and sadness.

"That's impossible," she replied. "The Garem are long gone. No trace was found of them, here or up there." She remembered the cries of the parents, searching the canals and laneways for their lost children.

Jareth turned and shed his robes and shirt. A golden caul covered his back, beneath which was the nascent beating of wings. Mara gasped.

"The stories were all true. The new order of priests, they wanted to tame Sister Death. They were waiting for us, when we climbed down from the rooftops on the winter solstice..." He shuddered as he pulled his shirt on.

If gargoyles had tears to shed, she would have cried. "We were kin, the Garem and gargoyles. *We* are kin, Jareth." She grasped his hand. "The rumours were terrible. Vivisection, paring away wing-cauls. Taking their *essence*, decanting it, imbibing it."

Jareth put his arm around her shoulder and it felt like family. "That was how the Blackhearts were born. Remember, they left just one gargoyle" – he gestured to Mara – "and they also left one Garem, though I don't think it was deliberate. Now, the Blackheart is coming to finish their work."

Mara had no desire to be a heroine, but she was a gargoyle of ancient lineage. Protection was her birthright and her curse. In her hands, the book felt warm, alive. A relic of another time that had survived the worst excesses of men and their desire for power. What was in those three missing pages?

Footsteps, fleet and light, echoed through the streets of Undercity. A shift of otherworld breeze whispered past them, then blew into the darkness like the ghosts of night birds. *L'Empire de la Mort must be close,* Mara thought, given that the corpseroad led right into Undercity.

"How did the Blackhearts want to tame Sister Death?"

Jareth gently touched Mara's cheek, then let his hand rest for a moment on the Book. "He is like you and me, the last of his kind. After I came here, the Boatman who ferries souls across the river of stars would often sit with me and tell tales of what had gone before. What was to come. He told me that when the last of the Blackhearts came to the river, he could finally rest, for *that* man would be coming for his wife…"

Mara wrinkled her nose; she had never had a taste for cryptic answers. What kind of wife would someone's soul make? And why would that be so dangerous for—

Oh. The horror of it turned her cold. "The Blackheart is coming to take Death for his wife," she said.

"*The envy of the devil, Death entered into the world.*" The Book whispered.

"And he who controls Death," Mara said, "controls the world."

* * *

In all her years on the rooftops of her city, Mara had seen more of Death's minions than she cared to remember. Red Caps, swarming through the city after it was invaded by the forces from the north, drinking the blood of the fallen. Deathwatch beetles, clicking through the houses of the plague-ridden populace, ticking down the time they had left. Sparrows unstitching souls from bodies with gentle beaks. Although never Sister Death herself, only the strange, creeping penumbra her robes left behind on the cobbles and at the river's edge. Death only came for certain occasions. She had minions in their thousands for the menial task of ending ordinary lives.

Death, it was rumoured, preferred to stay in her land, and wait for the windfall souls to turn it the green and silver of eternal spring, as they rushed from the Boatman's interminable tales.

They had decided Mara would be safe if they waited at the Endless Well. And, if all else failed, they could try to toss him in there, to fall forever. "Not much of a plan," Jareth admitted, "but it's the best we've got."

So, they hid in the gloom around the well, beneath the knotted and gnarled roots of trees that grew up through the high ceiling of Undercity and plunged through the earth below. The roots were studded with skulls of indeterminate creatures and Jareth whispered to them, listening to the clacking of their jaws as they spoke back.

"Do they all pass this way then?" Mara asked. The path that souls took had never concerned her. As a gargoyle, she would never tread it herself.

Jareth shook his head. "It's not a thoroughfare, as such. The Endless Well is just that – however, if someone navigates it, rather than falling through it, it can be a gateway to the Land of the Dead. For the Blackheart, who is neither alive nor deceased, there is no other way."

Mara stroked the cover of the Book again, ran her finger gently down its spine. She opened it, her touch clumsy and heavy. *The stone is taking root,* she thought.

"Do you think he's scared of what is to come?" she asked.

"Men – *creatures* – like him fear everything."

How could a Blackheart know what real fear was? Mara had spent decades living in fear, the feeling of it constantly, gently choking her as surely as the iron chain they made her wear around her throat. She had never done anything as terrible as they did, in their desire to master their fear.

Didn't you? asked a small voice inside her. She remembered the knife in her hand, the heft of the hammer as she nailed him to the cross.

"I'm not like them!" she said aloud.

Jareth turned and looked at her questioningly. Then he smiled. "No, you're not." As though he knew exactly what she had been thinking. "Neither of us are."

The Book rustled in her lap, as though it were agreeing with her. She looked at it for a moment, turned it over in her hands.

"Jareth, where do you think dead books go?"

"Dead books?"

"The things of this world – and others – that don't breathe, are not necessarily dormant. They need only exist for long enough, to be touched by enough of those that do live, in order to become living things themselves. The masonry of cities built upon, torn down, built up again; the forged metal of swords drinking up the blood and gore of a thousand slain foes; books, worn soft by countless leafing, whose words are a bottomless well from which reader after reader drinks, yet never runs dry. This imbues them with life. And to all that lives, Death comes eventually, yes?"

Mara knew this, as surely as she knew her own skin.

Jareth had the good grace not to laugh at her, although his eyes made him look as though he certainly wanted to. "Here," she said, beckoning to him. She held the Book out to him. As soon as it began to slip from her grasp, her arm felt heavy, almost too heavy to move. She wrenched it back just in time.

"It might be the Book that is keeping me from turning completely," she whispered.

Jareth nodded as she reached for his hand and held the Book flat in her other palm. Mara placed his hand on the cover. Together, they opened it and the paper rippled.

"It is almost as though it has a life of its own, no?" she asked. He sat next to her and turned to the missing pages. He jumped when she placed his fingertips on the edges left behind. He had felt the same thing she had.

"It's like an unhealed wound," she said. "And those pages, they no longer exist. Whether he burnt them or tore them to shreds, they are no longer in this world. I can feel that, too. So, perhaps…"

"You think that they are in the Land of the Dead?"

Mara nodded. "If I get there before he does, I can get them back and we can finish the spell. Then he won't be taking anyone for a wife. Certainly not Death!"

"I don't know," Jareth replied. "There is an awful lot that can go wrong with you going…*there*."

"There is more that can go wrong by fighting him *here*. Unless we finish the whole spell, we may never be free of him."

The skulls garlanding the tree branches chattered, their teeth clattering together like a hollow choir. A cold breeze blew along the path and the light flickered like the last of summer fireflies.

"He has entered Undercity," said Jareth, his face grim.

"You need to hide! He cannot find out you…"

"He does not know—"

"I think he knows a lot more than we anticipated. You need to protect yourself. And I need to make sure I am well ahead of him. Go!"

Book under her arm, she sprang down the mouth of the Endless Well.

* * *

Mara climbed down the walls, sharp claws clinging to the cracks in the brickwork, looking for the byway to the Land of the Dead. Her gargoyle eyesight was unable to penetrate the darkness. It was weighted, and it wanted to pull her in. She stopped, breathing deeply, and gripped the walls tighter. Far below, a chink of light broke the darkness. She clamped the Book between her teeth – what she wouldn't have given for a bloody harness to hold it! – and raced for the light, scared that it would disappear.

It shone through a tiny crack in the wall. She wiggled her claw through it, moving it back and forth. The fissure widened and she pulled the stones away, letting them fall into the emptiness below. Soon enough, it was big enough for her to slither through.

She found herself in a chamber, not unlike Undercity. Although this was much older. Crude carvings lined the walls, and she could hear the sound of water rushing somewhere far below. The light came from the moss that grew in patches on the walls. And the stone itself…it spoke to her, in a language she didn't readily understand, although it had a slow, steady rhythm.

"Sorrowsong!" she said aloud. Words, music, life, and time soaked into the stones of a city, folding into music that few could understand. For gargoyles, sorrowsong was like oxygen. Here, in this ancient place, she felt utterly drawn to it. Here, life and death were the same. *If I stay here,* she thought, *I will become one with it.* That was enough to set her to scampering across the cavern, to the arched doorway on the other side.

Down, down, down, the air growing colder and the whispering voices entreating her to stay awhile, to listen to their tales. To drink in the time that was seeping out from them: eons tiding, being pulled by her presence, the same way the ocean is pulled by the moon. Each chamber she went through was older than the last; each language they spoke in more ancient than the one before. It was as though she was passing through the layers of the world and all the years that had laid themselves down upon it, like peat.

She held the Book to her tightly. If she let go, even for a second, the stones would claim her for their own. As she stepped into a chamber that was covered in ammonite fossils, the sound of the rushing water abruptly grew louder, shushing the voices. The cavern narrowed into a tunnel that smelled of dampness and decay. Turning a final corner, she came upon a plain wooden door with a skull-shaped handle of glittering jet black that turned under her touch. The door swung open, and Mara walked through, onto the banks of a silvery river that smelled like the stars in summer.

Fog swirled over the opposite bank, obscuring any landscape. The bank on which Mara stood was only a thin stretch of land between the river and the huge wall running alongside it. Ahead, the wall and the river both curved out of sight. Mara put her hand on the wall; the rough bricks from which it was made were so old that the voices in them were sleeping. She worried about Jareth; was he alright, had he hidden himself well? She could only hope and do what she had come here to do.

Taking the Book gently between her teeth, she began to climb, claws digging into the crumbling mortar between the bricks. The rough wall felt familiar, somehow. It made her want to smile. "Not exactly an appropriate reaction to arriving *here*," she said aloud.

For although she had never been here before, there was no doubt that this was her destination: the river running smooth and dark, perfect for the Boatman and his endless cache of tales; the light that was darkly bright, the blue of a healing bruise; and the hush that ran through everything and settled in Mara's mind. This was no place for the living.

It felt like no time had passed before Mara's hands gripped the parapet and she hauled herself up onto the very top. She took the Book from her mouth and hugged it to her chest, looking down on the land within the walls. Over her not-inconsiderable lifetime, she had heard stories too many to count about the Land of the Dead. Clearly none of them had been told by anyone who had ever been here.

Below her spread out a city, entirely enclosed by mediaeval walls, twenty feet thick and covered in trees so ancient, it made the world seem young. The city itself was a maze of cobbled streets, jade-coloured parklands, and buildings that didn't look as though they had been constructed, but grown from the ground itself. The streets and laneways slowly turned and reconfigured themselves, so that it would be impossible for one who was walking those streets to retrace their path. The whole city was lit with thousands of tiny lights, strung across it in haphazard patterns. And despite the silence of just moments before, outside the wall the city sounded livelier than she had ever heard.

"Noisy bunch, aren't they?"

Mara turned, almost dropping the Book. "Who's there?"

"Apologies, dear gargoyle, I sometimes forget myself." The shadows gathered together and coalesced, as though unseen hands were sculpting them into the folds of robes, thin elegant hands, a tall marble masterpiece of the feminine form. Mara felt clunky and somewhat inadequate by comparison.

"Sister Death."

"The very same." She smiled, and it had only the hint of a rictus grin about it.

It was unexpectedly reassuring. Mara smiled back. "My name is Mara. I wouldn't have believed that *L'Empire de la Mort* was a walled city. How is it big enough for…well, all the dead?"

"Walls do not necessarily constrain, Mara, but they do define."

Mara thought about the red rooftops that were her home, the walls inches and feet thick that kept the people safe. "And they are built to keep out more than to keep in," she said.

Sister Death nodded. "You have found your way here, despite being very much alive. I am very interested to know why you have come."

Mara held up the Book. "I am looking for your library."

* * *

The entrance was a map room, filled with enormous globes covered in land masses, depictions of sea monsters and daemons of the air; maps that showed a flat earth, ending in a tremendous waterfall and ships falling off the edge; city maps of Atlantis, Babylon, Asgard. People dressed in garb from all the ages walked from map to map, some arguing with one another and furiously jabbing at maps to make their point.

"The cartographers can never see eye to eye," Sister Death whispered as they passed through the hall. "Some of them have been arguing for what must be centuries in your time." She made no sound as they walked the marble floors, and Mara tried to keep her footsteps light, conscious that she sounded like rocks tumbling through a river.

Earlier, as they had made their way to the library, turning down laneways and leaping across rooftops – well, Mara leaping, her host thinning to a sliver of shade passing through the air – she had explained His Eminence's plan to Sister Death, who stopped atop a verdigris cupola, her face grave. Mara replayed Sister Death's words as she led Mara through double doors and into the library proper. *I have battled and bargained with the Blackhearts for a long time. If he reaches here, I would be unable to refuse his proposal. It is not a prospect I relish. I never thought this time would come...*

Mara had not dared ask why she could not refuse.

As they stepped into the library proper, all else was forgotten. It was a huge, round tower, bookshelves lining all the walls. Lit by the ghosts of gaslights, it was so tall that the topmost shelves disappeared into darkness. People climbed ancient wooden ladders and scampered across the shelves, sorting, removing, replacing. They spoke to one another in whispers like the rustling of parchment. Mara's knees felt weak and she reached out for Sister Death's bony arm.

"How am I going to find what I need in all this?" The Book pressed itself to Mara's chest. It was scared, perhaps in the same way a human would be if they suddenly found themselves surrounded by innumerable corpses. She stroked the cover.

"It should find you," the Sister replied, gesturing for Mara to open the Book.

The gargoyle crouched to the floor, and balanced the Book on her knees, opening it to the missing pages. She made herself as still as if she were perched atop the cathedral keeping watch over the city. Taking a deep breath, redolent of the scent of old paper, papyrus, and vellum, Mara cleared her mind and closed her eyes. She waited.

Words in tongues long-forgotten drifted through her mind like sorrowsong. They pulled at her gently, children vying for a parent's attention.

It has been so long since we've been heard, they said.

She let the words wash over her, sluicing her in story. Then, a falling snow of pages against her skin – fragments torn from tomes, scraps that no one missed, book leaves whole and intact with ragged edges, floating and flurrying toward her.

The Book heaved a sigh, just as a dog might when it is settling to sleep. Mara opened her eyes, expecting to be half-buried in mounds of discarded words. There was nothing except the marble floor and the Book on her knees. She held her hand over the open Book. There, against her skin – the spectre of the three missing pages, reunited with the Book.

"Bugger," she said. Knowing they were now there was one thing – *reading* them when they were not visible was something completely different.

Her skin prickled unpleasantly. The library was no longer filled with the librarians' murmurs. It was too silent. Too still, even for a gargoyle. Sister Death laid her hand on Mara's shoulder. "I'm afraid that may be the least of our problems."

The clank of an iron collar made Mara's blood run cold. She turned.

Behind the Lady stood the Blackheart, smiling despite his scarred lips where he had torn the stitches Mara had sewn before his crucifixion. At the end of the chain in his hand, fastened by the collar, was Jareth, his face bloodied.

"I would have called out to you earlier, my pet," the Blackheart growled, "but I first needed to find myself a new tongue."

* * *

Betrothal is a curious thing and it would be easy, Mara imagined, to accept a proposal that you thought would never come to fruition.

Even Death sometimes makes mistakes, the Lady told her as they waited at the library door for the streets to reconfigure, so they could step through to her grand chamber at the heart of *L'Empire de la Mort*. The Blackheart held Jareth's chain tightly. Blood oozed from the corner of his mouth and Mara felt sick. It was *her fault* he had been injured so brutally. The appearance of the Blackheart, twice as tall and strong as her, with a wingspan that blocked out the light, had drained the last of the hope that she had.

"I admit I was expecting something entirely different, my Lady," the Blackheart said. The sounds of revelry came from all sides. "Why, it sounds like quite the party down here."

"If the Land of the Dead is not to your liking, you would be wise to rethink your desire to marry me." Her tone was dry as bleached bones.

They stepped through the doorway, into the grand chamber. From the high, vaulted ceiling hung an enormous orrery of all the different worlds over which Sister Death presided; human, fae, borderlands. It moved in complicated, transecting circles, making Mara dizzy.

"No wonder you send your creatures to do your work for you," she whispered to Sister Death, who smiled tightly in return.

The chamber was lined with niches in which dragonflies, crimson, azure, gold, appeared, clasping bright points of light in their pincers. They hovered in the hall, releasing those tiny points that blossomed into shimmering shades of all manner of things now extinct, then faded, leaving behind the scent of sandalwood and rosemary.

The Blackheart growled and muttered. Mara turned as he tried to swat at the dragonflies that hovered above him, just out of reach. Despite herself, she wanted to laugh.

"Is it true that dragonflies weigh the souls of the dead?" she asked the Lady.

"It is. They also do so much more. In your world, you have *memento mori*. What they are doing here is our *memento vita* and—"

"Enough!" said the Blackheart, pulling Jareth toward a huge seat of smoke and bone – the throne of Sister Death. "Now, we have our bride, our groom, and our witnesses. We must do this properly, yes?"

Mara hugged the Book tighter. The Blackheart grinned and she shuddered. "Ah, yes, that vile tome. We'll not be needing that any longer, will we?" As he reached out, Mara twisted away and tried to run. He grabbed her by the throat, holding her firm.

Jareth cried out and grasped at his iron collar. Sister Death hissed. The Blackheart did not turn, only tightened his grip on Mara. "It's just a book, my pet, and it has done what I needed it to do. Why so loyal to the very thing that proved your downfall?"

He stared at her, in the same way he had when he had been His Eminence and she his pet. Although she had been able to hide certain things from him – her nights on the rooftops, watching the city and stars, sneaking to the choir rehearsals, restoring the Book – it was not in a gargoyle's nature to lie.

"Without it, I will be turned to stone," she whispered.

His eyes widened and he loosened his grip. A flare of sorrow brightened his eyes for just a moment and Mara relaxed. "There was a time I wanted to love you," she said.

Unexpectedly gentle, he laid his hand on Mara's head. "And I you, Mara." His hand dropped to her cheek, then, lightning quick, to the Book. "However, that time has passed."

He wrenched the Book from her grasp and threw it to the ground. Emptiness filled her and Jareth dropped to his knees beside her. He stroked her skin and her wings. The Blackheart shrugged and looked down at Sister Death as she shouted furiously at him. Mara could not hear her voice.

With one last, great sigh, Mara closed her eyes and gave herself over to the stones. It should have been unpleasant. Instead, it was like being warmed by a fire in the winter or listening to the stories of her kin. It felt like coming home.

Perhaps here, in the Land of the Dead, among the memento vita *is where I was always meant to be.*

Time stretched across all boundaries. Movement ceased to have meaning. She waited to fade away, to be filled instead with the voices and memories held in the millennia-old rock. Instead, something fluttered against her left arm. *I should not be able to feel anything,* she thought. Then, the same on her right arm, flittering and *wrapping* itself around her. Then a third, on her chest, soft as spring rain. Instead of the voices of the stones, a different, familiar voice.

You found us, and bound us, kept us safe from harm.
He separated us from our kin, shred us and burned us.
And you found us again, down among the dead words
Forgone worlds.
You found us again…

The ghosts of three missing pages! Mara's flesh tingled where they lay against it. She imagined leafing through the Book to them and seeing what was written there, for they were reaching out to be seen and read. She only saw a random series of diagrams and sketches, words that jumbled and turned. He must have removed these even before she discovered the Book, for they triggered no memory, no recognition.

Here, a sketch of one of the lost children, golden wings open and glorious against a wide sky. There, spell words in an unfamiliar language, and a sketch of the hemlock plant. The next page, a lock of dark hair curled and pressed in the top left-hand corner, surrounded by the chemical symbols for water, oxygen, iron. There were crosses and prayers, formulas for elixirs and drafts, yet more spells to call, to banish, to bind. If she had a year, she would not be able to make head nor tail of it! In the lower left-hand corner of the penultimate page was a sketch of the Blackheart standing tall, surrounded by a strange light and Sister Death, pressed against that light and unable to get close to him. Then the final; a dragonfly, in all its delicate glory, and a set of scales. Nothing more.

We are the remains of possibility,
The garden through which you must draw a path,
Hidden, in plain sight.
We are string through the labyrinth…

Their tone was insistent.

Oh! The images flashed through her mind again as the pages clung to her and whispered encouragingly. They did not contain instructions, or even a set of directions as to what *must* be done after crucifying His Eminence. They were clues as to how to stop the Blackheart if he came into being! A shield, to be transformed and sharpened into sword. Mara's heart lightened. *This* had not been her fault after all.

She turned the images over in her mind, lifted them from the parchment and laid them in new permutations, one after another. Arrange, rearrange, repeat. Then the pages stopped speaking. Mara opened her eyes.

Sister Death and the Blackheart stood before the throne with a Red Cap (of all things), who looked to be acting, most reluctantly, as marriage celebrant. The murmur of speech, the sound of Jareth's breathing reached her, although it sounded as though it were filtered through a great body of water from far away. Jareth remained slumped on the floor beside Mara, his eyes turned towards the ceremony. The Blackheart held the end of the chain attached to Jareth's collar loosely in his hand. The dragonflies had stopped their flight through the hall, and were perched on the walls, still as the grave.

Softly, softly, Mara spoke through the stone, calling to Sister Death's tiny brethren, whose wings shone with light from the worlds above and whose pincers were strong enough to remove a soul from a living body. Since she very much doubted the Blackheart was now in possession of a soul, she needed them to use those pincers for something else.

Three, four, five dragonflies took flight, wending their way toward Jareth. Mara hoped against hope that they were soundless. They landed on the link between the collar and chain. Jareth looked over at Mara, his eyes widening when he saw her looking back at him. He brought his hand up to the iron chain as the dragonflies did their work. Snick, snick, snick; the chain fell away and Jareth gripped it tightly.

The bride and groom, such as they were, were faced toward the sulky Red Cap. Jareth rose into a crouch and signalled to Mara to do the same. There wasn't enough movement left in her, and all she could do was widen her eyes and give a tiny shake of her head. Jareth nodded and leapt forward, throwing the chain around the Blackheart's neck. Squealing, the Red Cap leapt behind the throne. Jareth tightened the chain; the Lady stepped forward, raising her slender hand to the Blackheart's forehead. Try as she might, Sister Death was unable to touch him, and Jareth's chain was having little effect.

Mara pulled the sorrowsong toward her, composed of all that time had left behind in the stones: the stories told by the innumerable footsteps in the cobbles; cities built up layer on layer of streets, houses, temples; cities razed by fire and war, burnt and destroyed and rebuilt again. The residue of life that flowed, slow and smooth, within them. While the Blackheart and Jareth struggled, while Sister Death circled them, looking for a way to bring her endless sleep upon her would-be groom, Mara silently called on the memories of the gargoyles and the Garem. Of their lives and their ruin at the hands of the Blackhearts.

All this she drew upward, upward, into her belly, her heart, her marrow, and then wailed it outward. The earth beneath her cracked and fissured, and the Blackheart staggered, his foot wedging in one of the crevices. The ceiling was abuzz with dragonflies, all carrying tiny, golden orbs of light, humming their own wordless tune. About the long ago love between humans and gargoyles that lived in them; about Sister Death opening her lands to them, making them kin; about the bravery of the gargoyle Mara, who had the courage to befriend the Lady instead of fear her.

The insects hovered over the Blackheart as he desperately tried to free himself, dropping those orbs as though scattering pearls from a pirate's chest. They streamed over his skin, tightening around him in a net of liquid gold filament, holding him fast. Mara whispered her sorrowsong to the stone, a story of the awful treasures that resided in the Blackheart, waiting to be mined. And it freed itself from her flesh, flowed from her like magma and rose up the Blackheart's calves, his thighs, torso, shoulders, as the golden net lifted and scattered in the air. He only stopped screaming when the creep of mineral and ore and rock reached his throat. It continued to rise and he stopped struggling, and was nothing more than a statute that might have been carved by a demented sculptor.

Mara was shaking as Sister Death and Jareth ran over to her. Sister Death placed the Book in her arms. "He and his ilk never did understand that I, and my land, are something to be embraced, not tamed. Instead, they're instilled with no more courage than a weasel." She reached down to pull Mara to her feet.

Jareth embraced her and she felt, perhaps, she had at last found a brother. She gently touched his lips. "I'm so sorry."

Sister Death shook her head, her face disgusted as she looked over at what used to be the Blackheart. "It's just a pity you didn't have the chance to sew *his* lips shut this time."

Mara smiled. "I always did hate a screamer."

* * *

The gargoyle, Mara, sits atop the red roofs of her city, watching time pass and lives run their course. She cannot leave the rooftops again; would not even if it were possible, for she carries the Land of the Dead with her. It ripples under her skin, a scar's delicate ghost. Nothing like the memory of the iron collar, which has faded so that, most days, she forgets she ever wore it at all.

Jareth, his shining wings no longer hidden, brings her sweetmeats from Undercity and rocks that the dragonflies leave at his door. His tongue is beginning to heal and, although he no longer can speak to Mara, they share a language that does not require words. Sometimes, when the moon is slung low in the sky, he wraps an arm around her, and she sings those rocks to life. Sculpting new gargoyles that leap on her back and scamper down the drainpipes. *One day*, she and Jareth think together, *there may be more Garem…*

Then they turn back to the city, and the life unspooling there, as Sister Death and her minions dance through the streets, gathering the world's dusk and its souls, the remnants of life, making room for all that is to come.

the wheel sings to us both

After so long in the dark, Ever craved pretty, useless things. Carriages of gold, twisted into the shapes of mermaids and fallen angels; lakes of swans, flanked by goddess statues; endless feasts tasting of summer. She soon realised, though, that carriages of gold and sweet feasts could never fill her up. No, she needed *people*. Something from each of them would make Ever happy. For a while, at least.

A girl like Ever is never full.

That was why she needed Whiskey-Kate.

Ever was pieced together from the remnants of other lives. Little girls like Ever aren't born and they don't die. The makings of them lay in wait in the woods, underground, laced out in unsettling patterns. Like mushrooms waiting to bloom at the first lightning storm or cold breath of autumn. The voices of forgotten things.

When the things once known and now unknown burrow deep down and find those makings, little girls like Ever wake up. But this time, she would seek out Kate, and make sure she never had to lie in wait again.

* * *

The ruins of the orphanage stood in the midst of the green-lit woods, crumbling walls covered in verdant moss and twisted weeds blooming purple flowers in spring. Time hadn't touched the old foundling wheel though, still in its place in the remains of the west-facing wall. Whiskey-Kate stopped and lit a cigarillo, looking the wheel over carefully. "I must be mad," she said, pulling the crumpled paper from her pocket. The old woman she had obtained it from had seemed genuine enough. *This is the spell that will open the doorway for you.*

Kate shook her head, trying to dismiss the thought that this was ridiculous. This was where she had been found, after all. She knew of other such baby hatches, but had never seen another quite like this one. Instead of a revolving crib set in the wall, the wheel was as tall as a man, made of dark stone veined with pale gold. At belly height, an opening revealed a hollow space, its floor dipped to cradle an infant. After placing the bundle inside, the mother would pull a rope, which rang a brass bell and activated a hidden mechanism, turning the wheel to deliver its cargo to the nuns on the other side.

Kate could have sworn that odd shapes had covered its surface, runes or an old language now faded from memory. That morning, though, it was smooth, innocuous. It felt like a bad sign, but she began to read the old woman's words aloud, trying to connect with the history of this place. Her history.

In days gone past, when bread was scarce and winter iced the streets of the hilltop town above, the wheel was used constantly to deal with the babies whose hungry mouths their mothers could ill-afford. Better, they thought, than to abandon them on church steps or throw them into the dark, swift river. Babe after babe was bundled into that tiny space, the bell rung as quietly as possible.

They were all orphans adrift on the tides. Whiskey-Kate knew it all too well – a feeling of being anchorless that could only come from knowing you'd been left alone in the world, unwanted from the moment you were born.

The orphanage had been abandoned for decades when the woman who became Kate's adoptive mother found her in the baby hatch one winter morning. "You were swaddled as though in a wee cocoon, still warm despite the winter. The runes were shining bright that day, as though saying you'd been left just for me."

That didn't explain where the story came from that Kate was a changeling, left in the wheel by the fae. But all her life, Whiskey-Kate knew she didn't belong. There were things that she could do – trade trinkets for dreams, and grow or wither plants at her whim – that made her wonder about where she really came from. For so long, she had needed to find her roots and feel solid ground beneath her feet.

A blackbird called out and a tiny trickle of sweat ran down Kate's neck. She stopped reading and screwed up the paper, dropping it on the ground. The spell that she had been assured would lead her to the fae world had done bugger all. Just like trading dreams and running a market filled with otherworldly goods hadn't brought her any closer to finding what she craved.

If it *was* a doorway for the fae, it was only one-way. It made her uneasy. She might not be able to get through to the other side, but she had the suspicion that if she tarried here for too long, something may certainly come through to her. She stamped out her cigarillo and reached out toward the wheel. Before she touched it, it began to slowly spin. An ornate "E" shimmered silver on the surface before dissolving and running down it like rain.

Heart thumping, Whiskey-Kate waited, but the wheel simply rasped to a stop. Cursing, she turned for home.

* * *

Blackbirds twittered and took flight as Whiskey-Kate veered from the path, branches and brambles moving aside at her touch. She paused in the shadows as she reached the edge of her market and lit another cigarillo, listening absentmindedly to her stallholders' chatter.

"I heard that the three of them were seen dancing around the ruined orphanage at dawn!"

"Now, that's not your drunk husband telling tales again, is it, Iris?" There were howls of laughter as Iris blushed.

The juice man, Seb – as round and lovely as the fruit he sold – shook his head. "I saw them too. Just today, in my orchards."

Kate could almost feel them all holding their breath. The tales of the three goblin-girls had been around for as long as she remembered; even she felt a thrill, thinking they may have been so close.

"All three of them. I chased them away, but the way they looked at me..." Seb shivered. "The tree that they'd been picking from – well, all its leaves were turned like autumn and the trunk was covered in frost. And there was a chill breeze left behind, just a whisper of it..."

Laughing, Whiskey-Kate walked into the knot of stall keepers, shaking her head. "Worse than a knitting circle, you lot. Really, three kids walking past an old orphanage or pinching oranges does not a mystery make."

Seb produced a note, sealed with silver wax. "Maybe not, Kate. But they left this behind and it's addressed to you."

Whiskey-Kate took the letter, made to crack the seal then stopped. "You've got customers to serve," she smiled.

As they walked away, she opened the note, read it once, fumbled for her cigarillo packet, read it again. It was an invitation from Ever, mother of the three goblin-girls, to go into the centre of the woods the next day. It promised a way back to the fae side of the wheel. An inexplicable seed of fear unfurled inside Kate.

"Why is it always the goddamn woods?" she mumbled. "Would it be too much to ask for this sort of thing to happen, just once, inside a good pub?"

* * *

Pushing aside late-blooming creepers, Whiskey-Kate stared at the small palace in the clearing ahead, a forgotten building from centuries before when the woods were part of the vast grounds of the royal family's estate. The royals had long since been deposed, the castle now a museum and its attendant buildings scattered through the woods, mostly left to crumble and rot.

But this building looked fresh, inviting – windows intact, shallow steps leading up to the French doors swept, a thin spindle of smoke rising from the chimney.

"She's put this on specially for you, you know." The voice was high, petulant. Dragging on her smoke, Kate looked up to the branches it had come from. A child of no more than five or six stared down at her.

"And you are?"

"Youngest. *Her* daughter," she replied, poking out her tongue.

"Ever's?"

Youngest nodded, swinging down through the trees.

"So you're one of those causing all the gossip in my market." Kate shivered as the child came closer, bringing a wintry chill with her.

"Don't let her kiss you!" A second voice, drawling and bored, came from another girl skipping from the shadows. Russet and gold autumn leaves framed her face. "Eldest," she said with a bow, then turned to Youngest. "Mother would have your guts for garters if you harmed our guest. And where is dearest Middle? You know she mustn't go off by herself, no telling where she will end up."

Youngest shrugged, wrinkling her nose as she crawled back up the tree.

As Eldest sized her up, Kate remembered the stories that the flower seller, Iris, had told over the years about three imps who roamed the woods disguised as waifs. *They never wanted to belong. The oldest one, with autumn leaves instead of hair – she would like to unwind you from yourself, like the notes of a sad symphony unspooling into nonsense. And the middle child, who moves quicker than the wind. She would like to chase you through the dark forest and across the cold plains until you can't run anymore. Until you can never run again. The last one is a child of the mist. She will find you in the cold and the damp, scented with warm earth and its buried memories. All she wants is to kiss you, just once, on the tip of your nose. That kiss will mark you for her larder.*

Kate looked back at Eldest. "And here I was thinking that you lot were just old wives' tales to scare children."

Eldest smiled. "That's the thing about old wives' tales, Kate. There's always more than a grain of truth there. Now come – let's not be late for your party."

The French doors opened. A flash that might have been a girl – Middle, Kate presumed – whisked inside, followed by Youngest with her slithering, creeping walk. Eldest held out her hand to Kate. It was as dry as paper and cold as snow. As Eldest gripped her hand, an awful sadness came over Kate, akin to grief. Her thoughts spun to the fae side of the foundling wheel, where peculiar folk danced under the mountain. Snippets of memory flashed across her mind, scraps of things odd and not entirely pleasant. A fierce storm that pulled birds from the sky. Children with odd coloured eyes and spindled fingers reaching through barred windows...

She wrenched her hand away. The sadness immediately receded.

"Interesting," said Eldest, the corner of her mouth turned up in a cruel smile. "You're more like Mother than I would have thought. Both old in young bodies. Both discarded things—"

"Take me to Ever."

* * *

Eldest led Whiskey-Kate into the palace's entry palour, wallpapered in white with delicate indigo whispers of flowers and dragons. It smelled of cinnamon and sage, and a sandalwood trunk sat under the window. Eldest opened it and waved Kate over.

"Choose one."

Inside were piles of rotting lace and moth-eaten silks, tattered and faded as rags. *Grave gowns*, thought Kate, imagining ladies entombed in crypts in their useless finery, rings encircling mummified fingers.

"I'll pass," she said.

Eldest tsk-tsked. "Mother *will not* be pleased."

"I'm not particularly concerned," Kate replied. It was almost true.

Eldest slammed the lid, shrugging.

A door opened and they walked through to a larger waiting room, painted lemon with silver friezes and dark paintings of dour men and their cowering dogs. A recessed daybed was dressed in the same colours, a chill wisp of breeze blowing from the wall behind it. Whiskey-Kate sat on the soft cushions. From beyond the wall, there was scuttling and moaning, as though something was dying.

Kate lit a cigarillo with shaking hands, closing her eyes to steady herself. Vivid images swam before her, reminiscent of the memories Ever evoked with her wintry grasp. An oversized swan swimming through frozen waters, breaking the thick ice like a ship's prow. Young Kate, wearing red shoes and matching bows in her hair, in a cart being pulled by two albino bats. A crow in a black cloak, carrying a satchel and umbrella, walking through a desert filled with rotting ship's hulks—

"Stop!" she said.

Eldest smiled thinly. "Forgotten memories aren't always pleasant, Kate, they can be a warning. You don't have to go on, you know. Just push that panel behind you and you can go back to your normal life." She giggled and wagged her finger. "But be careful not to take a wrong turn, for that could lead you to Youngest's larder."

Whiskey-Kate felt connected to those memories by a long, thin thread. It tugged, just behind her breastbone. At the same time, she thought of Seb's ruby apples, remembered the beauty of Iris' songs as she set out her flower stall each day. She would miss them if she were to leave.

"It's the curse of creatures of in-between places, of those who leave home and set themselves down elsewhere. They will always hanker for the *other*, never truly belonging anywhere," Eldest whispered. She almost looked sorry for Kate. "Go back to what you know, my girl."

Kate reached out toward the panel, suspended between what is and what could be. Then, the scratching and moaning and a thump, thump, thump against the wall. Something was trying to get out.

She snapped her hand back and stamped out her smoke on the floor.

"I didn't come down in the last shower."

Eldest scowled. "Don't say we didn't give you a chance." She began to hum, a sweet dirge that made Whiskey-Kate think of those women in the crypt, grave gowns blowing in death's breeze. A door that Kate hadn't noticed before opened up and she followed Eldest into the darkness beyond.

* * *

Ever took her time preparing to receive her guest. Oh, she would offer her choices, of course, but one must *direct* those choices. Ever knew that Whiskey-Kate was one of those little girls – oh, yes, there was still a little girl in there, she was sure of it – who was always looking for the way home.

So Ever would give her what she sought, but only in exchange for something very precious indeed. It was time for challenges. Games with those who *wanted* were far too predictable. Playing them was like reading the same story over and over again.

So, the costume of smoked glass or the black, trimmed with phoenix feathers? No, no, a dress that was also an ally, as it were. After all, Ever didn't trust Whiskey-Kate for a moment, any more than she trusted those wretched daughters of hers.

* * *

Chandeliers, sharp and icy, took shape in the darkness. Eldest had left Whiskey-Kate on a chaise lounge in the middle of a third, gloomy room into which light like dawn slowly filtered. It was a ballroom, pale blue, hexagonal, with ornate mirrors and silver friezes on each wall. Although she knew she was alone, the mirrors showed her something different.

In the first, great craggy mountains beyond a snow-filled plain lit by thousands of golden lanterns. In the next, a masked ball was taking place, the dancers wrapped in finery and jewels and feathered masks, under candles encased in floating glass baubles. Here, a beach empty but for an ancient piano being played by an old man, mermaids splashing in the shallows of the surf. There, a dark wood in which a feast was laid out on a long table, tall wraiths making their way through the trees to eat. And in the last one, a cemetery with tombstones and mausoleums and weeping women all green with moss and damp from drizzling rain.

A figure in grey wove through the crypts and statues, towards the mirror then through its silvered surface into the ballroom. Whiskey-Kate stood. "Ever," she said softly, nodding towards her.

The size of a ten-year-old, Ever's face was framed by a sweet, dark bob and undercut by a not-so-sweet smile. Swathed in a gown of old spider webs sparkling with droplets of rain and dotted with butterfly and dragonfly wings gleaming like raw jewels, she moved towards Kate the way a feral cat moves – stealthy and skittering and dangerous.

The web-skirts swayed and flowed, the light catching the wings in ghostly flutters. Ever looked Whiskey-Kate up and down.

"No gown?"

"I'm not really a gown type, dear."

"Or a *manners* type, clearly. Very well, I can dispense with pleasantries, if I must." Ever sighed, and pouted like a spoiled brat. "But I'm most glad you accepted my invitation. We've been waiting a long time, see, to be ready, and you're our final guest." She whistled softly and, in the mirrors, her daughters came into view: Eldest singing to the dancers of the masked ball; Middle skipping across the snow-plains like the wind; Youngest presiding over the ghostly feast in the dark forest. All dressed in the lacy grave dresses.

Whiskey-Kate felt the invitation in her pocket, reminding herself why she had come here. "As much as I'm…flattered to be your guest, I came because you offered to show me the way *over*. I'm supposing that word got to you in the same way as all the others…" Yet again, she found herself believing that this time, *this time*, would be the one. "I know how this is supposed to work. What do you want in return?"

Ever laughed; it was surprisingly pretty. "To come with you, of course!"

Kate sat down heavily on the chaise. "That doesn't make any sense!"

"I can't get there by myself."

"Well, you're not a hell of a lot of use to me then, are you?" she snapped.

The two women stared at one another, the figures in the mirrors looking on.

"We can help each other. I am an old scar, Kate, thousands of hurts and pains and angers cut deep then healed over. It's the foundling wheel, you see. Every time it turned, every cry and relief and guilt and horror that went with them, went into me. And then, when the orphanage was deserted and left to ruin, well, I needed other things to keep me alive. I sent my daughters out – capricious though they are – and they brought me back all manner of treats that kept me strong."

Kate knew the stories of people who would go missing for a few days, turning up with no memory of where they'd been, only flashes of songs and running and fear. If they turned up at all. "What kept you alive?" She tried to keep the contempt out of her voice.

Ever narrowed her eyes. "Interesting things…the sort of things that you must be brave to trade. A broken heart here, a love of song or stories there. Black secrets and blacker wishes – taking those away can break a person forever, unfortunately. But they're the ones who end up through there." She waved her hand carelessly at the mirrors.

Kate shivered and looked away. How many times had she traded similar things for the chance to get closer to the place she thought of as home? What would she trade now for the same chance?

"The wheel sings to us both then," she said. "But for different reasons, Ever. I might belong here, I might belong there, but I've never had the chance to find out. You are part of this place though, and I don't know enough about the fae side to know it's safe to take you over. Why do you need to go so badly?"

"Survival."

Quicker than the eye could catch, tendrils of spider silk snaked out from Ever's dress, piercing the mirrors and snaking towards her three daughters. They shrieked and ran, scattering dancers and feasters and sending up flurries of snow, but the tendrils followed them, weaving through the tattered lace of their frocks. They caught Middle last, a speck in the distance of the cold, white plain.

Kate stepped backward, fighting the urge to run as the web reached toward her too, and tried to spin around her ankles. But having no lace gown to weave itself through, it simply blew away like smoke. Ever drew her daughters in, wrapping the silk the way a spider wraps a struggling fly. It interweaved with the rotting fabric, winding it tight around their victims. Youngest and Middle whispered, *Please, Mother, no. Let us play just a while longer.* Eldest, though, kept singing, low and flowing and sadly discordant, a music so intimate that Kate felt as though it was running through her own head. As Ever wound her daughters closer and closer, Kate lost the feeling in her body, as though floating, disconnected above the ground. Drifting away from her very self—

"Shut it!" Ever cried, slapping Eldest on the face.

Kate came back to herself with a sudden heaviness in her limbs, the words of the stories echoing in her memory. *She would like to unwind you from yourself, like the notes of a sad symphony unspooling into nonsense.*

Eldest grinned at Kate, seemingly not bothered by the blood running from her split lip. She knows what she's just done, Kate thought. For Eldest's song had unwound the images from Kate's dreams, the memories that had flowed to her in the yellow room. Vividly sharp, the air froze her bare skin as her birth mother, shape-shifted into a giant swan, broke through the sea ice in their escape from the Fae-Queen's winter castle. Warmer now, her toes curled at the pinch of those red shoes and fear tightened her as the cart bounced along the back roads in the dark.

Despite the fear, the unpleasantness, it felt more real than life here ever had. An ache for home sat like stones in her chest.

Ever's laugh brought her back to the present. The spider silk had wound its way around her daughters' mouths and they had stopped struggling. Reaching out with her small, pale hands, she drew them closer and closer, the silken bundles shrinking until they were nothing more than folds of her gown. Flicking her skirt, Ever smiled. Eldest's hair of autumn leaves crowned her; the chill of Youngest's skin now emanated from her pale flesh; she moved towards Kate with the storm-swift gait of Middle and grabbed her wrist.

"My daughters have come home to me," she said, "and now we will come home to you."

The scenes in each of the mirrors had disappeared, replaced by an image of the foundling wheel, alone in the wood. The stones in Kate's chest shifted and grew heavier. She put her hand over Ever's.

"Yes. Let's go home."

In their silver frames, the wheels creaked to life and spun widdershins, eddying the air around Ever and Kate. Like a ball of wool unwinding, the wheels let go of all the grief, pain, and relief that women had found there. Babies left in the dead of night, the depths of winter. Children that they could not possibly feed; some, they could not possibly want, the offspring of assault and violence. Others, dearly wanted, but snatched from the mother's arms and dumped carelessly, to become someone else's problem.

The eddy pulled at Ever and Kate, drawing them together in the same way Ever's webbed skirts had drawn in Eldest, Middle, and Youngest. Ever grabbed tight onto Kate's other hand, put her face against her torso like a child hiding from the world. Kate closed her eyes and gave herself over to the memories that wound through her, making themselves whole again.

A vicious war waged for centuries between the fae tribes. Children from Kate's clan taken as slaves for the enemy. She and her mother escaping in the midst of a furious winter storm, in which even the birds had fallen from the sky, frozen mid-flight. Being captured and sent to the prison hulks of the Red Desert, patrolled by the caped crows who would choose child soldiers from among the prisoners.

But even among those fearsome corvidae there can be found decency and secret rebels. Kate felt soft, ebony wings carrying her to a place deep in the woods, where the sprites used spells to turn the time within her back, back, until she was a babe in arms again. They placed her into the foundling wheel and turned her through to the winter of this world.

Her mother had sacrificed *everything* so Kate would have another chance. The fae world was no home for her. Could never be her anchor. The stones of longing in her chest loosened to rubble and washed away as she tore her hands from Ever's grasp. "No."

The wheels scraped and slowed, as the air grew deathly still. "No?" Ever said. "You've already promised. You can't undo that. You can't *unknow* what it is that you want."

Whiskey-Kate reached out tentatively to take Ever's hand again, torn between her urge to go back to her roots, to find out where she came from, however ugly, and the need to honour the wishes of a mother she never knew.

She pulled her hand back again as Ever hissed and ground her teeth. The flesh on her face fissured, the cracks running down her throat and arms. What looked like spores puffed out from the gaps, floated toward Kate and swirled around her. The cracking deepened, widened until there was no more Ever. As the light dimmed, a clowder of pale, icy shadows surrounded Kate, whispering in Ever's old voice, in a language she didn't understand. The pale shades ran spindled fingers up and down her arm, pinching the skin on her wrists, the underside of her elbows. Each pinch felt as though *something* was being stolen from Kate, with memories of her past growing more vivid. The clowder coalesced, broke apart, pushed her towards the mirrors.

Bile rose in Kate's throat as Ever tried to unpick Kate's edges, to shiver her way into her skin, her body, and meld with her in the same way she had subsumed her daughters. Curling her toes into her shoes as though that would anchor her to the floor, her knees began to buckle. As she fell, she grabbed the bony wrist of the nearest shade. "Ever," she whispered. The clowder melded together again into Ever-whole, who shifted her arm and held Kate's hand, gently, gently.

"I know now, Ever, what it is that I come from. That's not something I can go back to…and that means there is nothing for you to hold onto either."

Whiskey-Kate squeezed Ever's hand; it crumbled into nothing. Without a scream, and with only the faintest look of surprise, Ever collapsed and disintegrated into a pile of soft, dark ash. A flight of amber moths rose from the ash and flew through the now-open door.

Sighing, Kate dusted off her hands, tucked her hair behind her ears. She was empty, exhausted, with not even enough left to cry for what had been lost forever. "Might be a good time to find that pub now," she said to no one in particular.

Following the flight of moths, she walked out into the late sunshine. There was a rustling in the trees as she walked down the steps, but when she looked, there was nothing there but shadow.

* * *

In the middle of the woods is a long-forgotten palace; parlour, waiting room, ballroom. The paint is peeling from the walls, and swallows nest in its darkest corners. A sudden wind, cold and snappish, blows through the broken windows, bringing a single autumn leaf with it. It settles in the corner, against a snow drift that hasn't melted since the last winter.

On the floor is a dark, oily stain. In the late afternoon light, it looks girl-shaped, almost plump, as though it is beginning to pull itself into form from the rotting wooden floors. In the still afternoon, the foundling wheel at the abandoned orphanage turns and calls out in its stony voice one, two, three times. A mouse ventures toward the oil stain, twitching its whiskers, investigating. The edge of the stain lifts and wraps around the creature. It doesn't have time to squeak before it disappears.

The dark stain plumps a bit more; the blue paint brightens a touch; the snow and the leaf lift and rustle. Not so far away, the wheel creaks again and it seems to whisper *soon, soon*, as though crooning to a waking child.

north, at the end of the world

Here, at the end of the world, we finches, and the kites, and the crows are one tribe. Symbiotic, the crows tell us. The kites have always lived here. This is their land. Their sky, stretching wide and hard blue in the dry season, heavy with grey clouds and fierce cyclones in the wet. We sing each other stories in the first light of dawn, about how the kites are born from that sky. That storm-eggs fall at the change of season and they crack their way out of them, fully formed and full of the hunter's terrible calm. That their sky is a cold place, despite the always-heat of this far-flung land. The cold from which they come makes the kites seek fire. Like salamanders, who crackle white and ashy through flame, their flesh is immune to it. How else could they pick it up in tiny pieces and carry it to do their work?

Today, the kites hunt. They wheel and drift on updrafts, dive toward the ground in arrows of feather and hollow-bone precision. Seeking out the ember and hot ashes of the fire in this desert scrub at the edge of the sea. The kites brave the smoke and pick up the smouldering fire-remains, carry them to a fresh, unburnt patch of bush, where their quarry hides. They drop the fire, wait for it to lick the dry trees, the ragged undergrowth. To flush out their prey. Once upon a time, we hid from their talons and the knife-curve of their beaks. We flew from their fire. But no longer; not here, at the end of the world.

Crows are our firestarters. They tell us much, but nothing of how they actually bring the flame. They hold their secrets close. But we swear that, at dawn today, we saw a murder of three flying with lightning in their beaks. It ran down their feathers like rain. Lightning and dry lands do not make good friends. Corvids have always been the clever ones, even when the world was whole, and especially when the world was breaking. Always seeking out survival, always adapting. Like the gangs of people who roamed the streets as the reckoning came about, they gather at dusk and mourn when one of them dies, and avenge those deaths in ways brutal and bleak. These are the same creatures who bring gifts to their mates, and tumble through the red desert sands in play. We cannot pretend to understand them, but we wish, sometimes, that we were like them.

We *were* like them once, in that we kept to ourselves, didn't need others to help us, or us to help them. Hiding among the blooms and leaves, in places none others could find, we have always been. Same as the crocodiles who slide through the muddy mangroves at low tide, eyes shining under the moon at midnight like windows into another world. The crocodiles and we birdlings share ancestry, hollow bones and vacant hearts remembering across millennia. But the crocodiles stopped singing long ago; they have lived the end of the world before.

This end of the world is tinderbox country, always ready to ignite. But we know its secret water holes, its streams that are cold and clear. That is one of our jobs, us finches. To direct the fire elsewhere, lest the water chokes in ash and soot. We fly, light and insubstantial as butterflies, finding those cool oases in the dry. Sitting on the slender branches, our bright blue feathers signal our kite brethren *not here*. They tell us we look like windblown buds, about to bloom. They tell us we look like life. It makes us happy, but it also makes us laugh.

For our other job is to find their prey.

At the beginning of the reckoning, the crows had headed north as the waters rose in the south, flying in great clouds of oil-slick wings and caws of the madness they had left behind. Now, all that is left here of the before-world is quiet ruination. Abandoned water towers, dry as bone and red with rust, slowly crumbling back into the desert sands. Airfields with silver planes, ghostly as the sun glints off wings that will never again know the sky. Desiccated bodies of humans who did not make it far enough, eye sockets and bellies empty, picked clean by the crows before the heat spoiled them. As we said, those crows are survivors. We did well to learn from them.

Today, as the kites soar and dip and carry fire that fills the sky with smoke, the king tides bring the sharks with them, browsing and brooding in the shallows. Singing to us of the southern land that is gone; of how the ocean swept through the streets and reclaimed it. Of underwater cities on which the salt has begun its work, and the bloated bodies that quickly became skeletons, garlanded with bladderwrack, periwinkles, sea stars. As we work, darting like quicksilver fish in the mangroves, we sing back about this wide, wild, northern land, where the bush stretches for miles, so far that land and sky never quite meet. Where the fires burst open seed pods, and after the rains the bush regenerates, vivid plumes of green against the grey ash-beds and blackened stumps. This land, we sing, listened to our ancestors; it made itself ready for the end of the world. It waited for us.

It waited for us and, all the while, the wind carried its wisdom. *Head north, north, at the end of the world*, pulling us finches, and the crows, the crocodiles and the kites, as inexorably as the moon pulls the sea.

As the moon pulls the sea, so, too, we three birdling-branches were pulled together to survive. Crow to start the fire, kite to corral it, finch to find the prey. Irony, that the prey headed north too, smart enough to follow those who had listened to the call of *north*. Not smart enough to know that the north is not for them. The land is not vindictive, but it is not kind either. So, beauty reminds them of better times, easier times. Of living in cities, of homes warm and dry. Of food they did not have to scratch from the earth or hunt, skin, gut. Of listening to birdling-song and making their own songs too. Beauty reminds them of all that they have lost. It is their weakness.

We finches are nothing if not beautiful.

This morning, as crows came with lightning and kites began their smoky flight, we flew and jumped in a wide corral, looking for people. Our prey. Finally, we found them camped in the trees, hiding from the heat, the insects, the kites that they know bring fire. One of the children, thin and ragged, sees us first, pointing at us, showing his mother and sisters. We sit quietly, heads cocked to one side, trying to look like the memories they so love. Now we flit, a flirty, pretty flight, through the undergrowth and the eucalypts, alighting on silvery branches and gently flicking our tails. The sunlight catches the blue of our wings, the white of our throats. More people come out of their hidey-holes to watch us and listen to our chirps. We watch back and find their secrets as if we were finding worms. Watching and patience. We know where they live now.

We sing it to the kites and the crows.

Today, the kites hunt. The flames take hold and the people flee from them, the same way that the possums and bilbies used to. It is better if the smoke gets them before the flames do, for their screaming makes us shiver. And while we don't have a taste for meat, the crows and the kites say the humans make for good pickings. They eat them like the crows used to eat toads – just the thighs, eyes, and intestines. We all take their hair for nests, for we try not to waste. The crocodiles make short work of the rest. All this time, the people keep coming north, in dribbles and drabbles that slow now. Their migration is almost done and, with it, our prey is nearly dried up like waterfalls in high summer. The people took everything once before, but we will not allow them to do that again. Not here, at the end of the world.

Here, at the end of the world, what was before unravels and turns back on itself. Those of us who were here in the beginning – the birdlings, the sharks, the crocodiles – are here at the end too. Today, as the kites hunt, crows and finches have a new job. We begin the search for new hunting grounds. New lands to reclaim. Crows know to always adapt, to seek survival; kites, that patience is the method of the hunt; finches, that, in the end, the strong need the likes of us as much as we them. A single crocodile, oldest and wisest of all, waits in the bay. On his back stand a crow, a kite, and a clutch of we finches. As the remaining kites hover in the smoke, and the sky turns orange from the flames, the crocodile slithers into the shallows and swims to the open sea, to places that our wings cannot take us. The finches' song, the crows' caw, the kites' cry, all carry across the waves. It is warning and hope and sadness, but also the language of beginnings. Beginnings, like green shoots from the ashes.

Heading north and singing out the future, in the hope that we can weave a world that does not end.

a solace of shadows

I was the first puppet the Marionette Master had ever made – the most imperfect, with one foot a little bigger than the other and a creaky right elbow – and so, the one closest to her heart. My auburn hair was upswept, dark eyes fringed with real lashes. I was not glorious, but I was hers. "Mereen, my little shadow," she would say.

It is an old tradition of the marionette masters – women, without exception, for centuries – to anoint their first creation with a drop of blood from their fingertip. It is an older tradition still to push boundaries and break the rules. So should it be such a surprise that she fed me with blood from her wrist? Or that she continued to do so, month after month as the moon waned and a frost of stars rimed the night sky?

I loved her as I would a mother. Like any child, I had my own secrets, my own broken rules. Although she sometimes wondered aloud at how her marionettes *almost* seemed to have minds of their own, she did not know that I fed them shadows, each and every night. I began because I wanted a family of my own, someone to provide for. But with those imitations of life inside them, their performances became riveting, and feeding them also became my way of repaying her.

So lifelike, the audience cried. *So inspiring*, the dowagers wept.

So creepy, the children whispered to one another.

* * *

Knights in metal armour, coloured feathers flowing from their filigreed helmets. Jaguars whose legs were permanently ready to pounce. Aristocrats in buckled shoes, raggedy hobos, plague doctors, dwarves heavy-pocketed with treasure. Moorish warriors with sharpened swords, angels and demons, and one enormous Cyclops. The more I fed them, the more marvellous the performances became. And the more feted the Marionette Master.

She lived at the theatre, on the upper floors, in a room draped with scarves, piled high with books, and an old, ornate mirror almost covering one wall. Outside was a garden in which she grew all she needed. Vegetables and fruit trees sprouting from the rich, dark earth. Herbs for flavouring and memory and to keep away bad luck. Chickens for eggs.

For my wooden family, each night a feast.

I waited until the crowd had filed into the theatre on the second floor, and the first notes of the old piano and the mournful violin began. Clack, clack, clack, my wooden feet on wooden floors, a snick of the lock, then out into the evening.

The garden shears lay on the potting table, the sun reflecting off them and onto the sandy-coloured brick wall, a replica in light. I reached up and carefully took down the light-shears that weighed no more than a feather. Nothing cuts umbrae so well as a sparkle of brightness. First, the shadows of sunset, long and rich, like a stew that has been simmering all day. Elongated tomatoes, thin crescents of eggplant, sheaves of rumpled cavolo nero, cut, cut, cut, then laid carefully in my basket of paper-reed. A bee had landed on the flowering thyme and, as the last of the sun slipped away, I gently scraped the subtle silhouette of the pollen clinging to his back legs, for a touch of sweetness.

Perhaps that little change was just what they needed. The jaguars and the warriors, in particular, had been restless of late, hard to fill, making me wonder if what I gave them was enough. The gentle harvesting calmed me. Darkness, then the bright, just-waning moon. Onto the moonlight-cast shapes – deeper, more substantial, limned in cold silver. The rosemary, like an oil stain, dark and strong-scented. Huge field mushrooms that grew in the loam near the back door, fresh-sprung from—

Something rustled through the fennel and parsley that grew wild behind the henhouse. Inside, the chickens cackled and cooed, undisturbed. I crept forward. A creak, a stealthy movement but not a sleek one, then a paw darted out, almost experimentally.

"Jasmine!" I hissed. The jaguar shook herself clear of the fennel and parsley patch, and at least had the good grace to look ashamed as she slunk over to me.

"I'm hungry, Mereen," she said, whiskers twitching.

"Well, I'm not out here for my health, you know! You'll get fed along with all the others after the show."

She shifted, her eyes darting across to the coop then back to me. "But they smell so tasty. Fresh meat. Blood..." Jasmine's eyes were fearful. "I'm not sure how I even *know* that's what I smell, but it's...irresistible."

I felt like a marionette whose strings had been suddenly cut. "Shhh now, you go back inside, and after dinner you'll feel as good as new. I'll take just a suggestion of some of the ham hock and blood sausage that's hanging in the pantry, what do you say?"

Jasmine nodded and turned back to the theatre. I finished collecting my ingredients in silence, all joy gone. Shadow-food should have been all that Jasmine – all that any of them – needed. But these days, even with the most elaborate meals, they remained hungry. As a last thought, I pinched some leaves of blueberry, basil, and rosemary from their stems and took them with me. If we were dealing with real desires, best have the means for an ancient protection.

For what if the silhouette-flavour of blood-sausage and cured meat wasn't enough for her? Or, worse, for any of them?

* * *

The single globe hanging from the pantry ceiling swung, the shadows it cast swelling and contracting. I didn't often use meat in my dishes, mainly because their shapes, against the pantry shelves and the jars and bottles sitting there, were so difficult to harvest. They were also unpredictable in the dishes, once having sent the Cyclops into a fortnight's slumber, another time causing the dwarves to run naked through the garden.

Waiting for the bulb to still, the scents of the food almost overcame me. Salt and sugar, the richness of passata in its jars and the earth clinging to the potatoes in their basket. They had never smelt so strong. But each time I fed on the blood of the Marionette Master, my senses sharpened. Where at first I could hear only *her* voice, now the voices of the hymn singers in the church two miles away woke me each Sunday. Where before had been the blurred shapes of patrons filing into the audience was now the detail of fabric and colour and movement.

I understood why Jasmine was creeping toward the henhouse and why there had been murmurs of dissatisfaction among the rest of my family. They had had the merest taste of what was possible, and it had made them hungrier still.

Against the dark of night, there was a perfect reflection in the pantry window of the ham hock, salted and cured over many months, hanging above the jars of olives and preserved lemons. The blood sausage hung next to it, dark and rich, curled over and over on itself. Was *this* my answer? Reflections. More than shadow, less than reality. *More than they are used to*, I thought. Caught in glass, these smaller, less substantial versions of the food could be perfect for what I needed.

I took my sharpest knife, bladed by morning sun on the kitchen wall and kept safe by lamplight, pressing it against the window. It didn't make a dint. I pressed harder this time, careful not to scratch the glass, digging the point into the reflected flesh of the ham. It yielded, just a touch, but it was for nought. My best knife, the one I kept for the most sharply defined, most stubborn penumbra, could not lift even the tiniest corner of the meat.

But reflection is more than shadow, less than reality. So I needed a tool that was more substantial than light, less than the crudity of a real knife. The reflection of a knife, perhaps? It would take me days to make one, to allow it to properly develop and blade. Then I remembered that earlier in the day, I had heard the tinkling of breaking glass. I went to the kitchen bin and carefully rummaged through it. A package wrapped in newspaper that crunched under my touch held the glass that I was after. I removed a shard and took it with me back to the pantry.

Again, I dragged the sharp point along the reflected ham. Nothing. Frustrated, I pressed harder. The shard slipped from my hand, my thumb nail running along the glass in its wake. Or, rather, *through* it. It had taken a tiny nick out of the reflection. I lifted my thumb again, tentatively carving first along the image of the ham, taking off a long sliver of fat and meat. Then along the blood sausage, gouging away a chunk. Afterwards, I licked my fingers, relishing the taste of flesh and blood and *sustenance*.

Newly acquired treasures tucked into my apron, I skipped back into the kitchen and began to cook. With my shining, insubstantial knives, I chopped the vegetables and herbs, popping them into the iron pot that had been warming on the hearth, the water inside bubbling gently. I had long ago discovered that trying to cook directly over the fire resulted only in a charred saucepan and ash, which does not a satisfying meal make. The warmth from the flames and their smoke was enough – that night, I used branches of applewood and pecan in the fire to flavour the soup. I stirred the shadows in and they drifted through the water like ink, releasing the colours trapped inside. Dark green of the cavolo reminiscent of spring forests; tomatoes the red of ocean sunrise; eggplant the shade of distant mountains shearing into the sky like knives. They held the memories of light as it travelled across the world. It carried more stories than we could ever tell, but we would feast on the world held in darkness and sunshine, giving life to our wooden limbs, our wooden hearts.

As the broth simmered, I tore the ham and sausage into small chunks. They were strange to the touch; not as fragile as the mere ghosts of food I was used to working with. My mouth watered and I could have happily stuffed myself with all those little pieces, leaving nothing for anyone else. I lifted a piece of the sausage to my nose, breathed in its earthy, coppery smell. *Just one piece*, I said to myself, opening my mouth.

A low growl from the corner stopped me. Jasmine's yellow eyes stared at me accusingly, as I put the piece down.

"I think I know how you felt at the henhouse," I said to her.

She nodded, then resumed her corner pose, watching me as I tipped the meat into the pot. The soup bubbled and spat and sheened with colour as the fat grew warm. One more stir, before leaving it to simmer and reduce for the next hour or two.

I left Jasmine purring in the kitchen, licking her chops, blissful in the warmth. In the pantry, I replaced my knives and spoon on the wall, dulled now from use, where they would catch the morning light. But something wasn't quite right. I sniffed. There was a whiff of something off that hadn't been there earlier. Nothing seemed out of place, none of the jars were broken. I sniffed again, then looked up.

The sausage, before beautifully dark and plump, was covered with a thin skin of sickly green mould, and the ham was wrinkled and desiccated at the edges. I tasted the sourness of the mould and it flooded me with shame. It was my fault, messing with something that I didn't fully understand. From the kitchen, the soft crackle of the flames reminded me of the simmering soup. I turned and ran out, intending to dash the pot to the floor. I grabbed the tea towel, ready to heave it off the hearth, when the smell wafted upwards. It was like nothing I had ever cooked before, earthy and salty and so close to *real food*, the kind that the Marionette Master ate. How could that be bad? Jasmine looked at me, curious. How could I deprive the others of a meal such as this?

Shaking, I returned the tea towel to its place and quietly shut the pantry door.

* * *

Through the windows of the marionette storeroom, the stars shone like sugar spilled on indigo silk. Ours was a small theatre, but we still took up the whole of the third floor, stored in rows and sitting against set pieces, the angels and skeletons and Death hanging from the rafters. That night's performance had been *Hansel and Gretel*, and applause rang through the theatre as Jasmine and I hoisted the soup up via the dumbwaiter.

Moving slowly in the starlight, my marionette family seemed from another time, another world. I was like them, yet not; I was the only one with the Master's blood in me. The only one somewhere between human and poppet. They stopped their chatter as steam from the soup snaked through the air. It made curious shapes, curling and wisping into the night.

"This is different, no?" Cyclops asked.

I nodded, ladling his share into a little wooden bowl. The others lined up behind him, shuffling impatiently. The more I ladled, the more soup there seemed to be. I pushed away the memory of the destroyed meats, hanging limp and straggly. I was just doing for my family what the Marionette Master did for me. I had no blood of my own to give, but I would still give them the best that I could.

Ladle, ladle, steaming broth
Like a candle, to a moth
Hanging on its heart's desire

Too close, dear moth, your wing's afire!

The skeleton marionette, Teo, stood back, plunking a tune on her ribcage and singing the words in time. She was the oldest of us all, having been left to the Master by her mother before her. I offered Teo a bowl, but she shook her head and walked away. Eccentric though she was, her tune unsettled me.

The rest of them slurped their soup, murmured to one another, to me, to the star points in the sky, that they had never tasted its like before. That it made the darkness seem darker and the memory of audience applause seem sweet and bitter, all at once. Their words blurred together, turned to a sibilant rhythm that sounded like joy. In the corner, the angel Aurora beat her wings and lifted a few feet off the ground. The rest of them laughed and someone put the old phonograph on, a snaking blues tune the Marionette Master would often listen to late at night.

I sighed, my uneasiness forgotten as my family revelled in their meal. I had given them more than they had had before and sated a hunger they didn't even know was buried inside them. But now I was hungry too, and I left them running their fingers around their bowls, licking the last of the juice from their fingers and dancing with one another to yesterday music.

* * *

The Marionette Master was waiting for me in her rooms above the theatre, curtains open to the night, as always. Outside, the landscape was silver and shade and patches of fog lying in wait in the valleys. She smiled at me, beckoned me over. "Mereen. My little shadow," she said.

I climbed up to where she sat on her bed, glass of wine in hand, and leaned against her, exhausted. She stroked my hair. "How I envy you sometimes, my little one. No past to reflect on, no future to worry about. Just right now…"

There is never just a right now, I wanted to say. Not once you've been fed. Not with the knowledge that comes from having the blood of another run through you, or from the need to feed others no matter the cost. I loved the Master, but at that moment, a snake-strike of hatred flared within me.

But I let her stroke my hair and murmur to me. What else was there for me? She put down the empty wineglass and opened the small silver case that held a pearl-handled straight razor. Pressing the blade to the soft flesh of her forearm she drew first a thin line of blood, and then pressed harder, crimson welling and running down her skin. I leaned forward, clamped my mouth over the cut and fed.

Under the initial spice of copper, her blood was sharp. It made me feel as though, but for that one night per month, I was indeed just a shadow, a vessel for delivering the desires of others. The audience, the Master, the marionettes. If I had teeth, I would have bitten down and sought the vein.

"Careful, now," she said, pulling me away from her. "This is enough, no? We are creatures of tradition, you and I, but we are not savages."

The Master wrapped her arm in a soft bandage. Before she had the chance to wipe my mouth, I used the back of my hand, then sucked the last drops from it. She picked me up, put me in the wicker chair by the window, so I had a view of the sleeping world outside and of her, reflected in the huge mirror propped up against the opposite wall.

The feed acted on me like the wine on her. From downstairs, there was a muffled shuffling as my family settled themselves to sleep. Beyond the window, the landscape and the streets were a thousand hues of black, and the sky above a raven's wing, feathers tipped with diamonds.

I drifted off to sleep, my Master already dreaming under her red quilt.

The nights I fed were the only nights I dreamed, and that night they were filled with creaking doors and huge cauldrons of steaming broth and my family whispering, *Hungry, hungry, hungry.*

I woke suddenly. In her sleep, my Master moaned. A movement in the mirror caught my eye – the corner of the red quilt moved once, twice, then was still. *Hungry, hungry, hungry...* The cry taunted me. It was a nasty sound and I wanted to curl up, put my hands over my ears. The door to the room, closed earlier, was now ajar. Jasmine's yellow eyes peered through. "We tried to stop them," she said, limping into the room. Her front leg was splintered, as though she had been in a fight.

The bottom right-hand corner of the mirror was cracked, opened as though someone had slipped through a break in an old fence. The reflection of the quilt rippled and twitched, but the actual quilt was still, undisturbed. I ran to the bed and ripped it to the floor, then turned back to the mirror. Marionettes – my *family* – swarmed over the Master's reflection. Aurora, Cyclops, the warriors and faeries and noblemen and women, all of them, feasting on it. They stripped the flesh away, plucked out her hair, scrabbled and fought over each of her limbs and the ripe roundness of her belly. Aurora tore the left hand clean away and, baring her teeth, flew into the corner of the mirror to eat. A soldier used his sword to cut away her cheek. And all the while, they all growled, *Hungry, hungry*. Jasmine whimpered and I was utterly paralysed. I could never have imagined there was such viciousness inside them. But *I* was the one who had fed them ghost-meat. *I* had awoken their need. I had failed.

Then I remembered the real meat, after I had taken only some of its likeness from the window. The mould. The decay. In the bed, the Master moaned and cried in pain. *They will never stop*, I thought. For there was no skeleton or viscera under the flesh they stripped away. Only the ghostly outline of our sleeping Master. Next, they would come for real muscle, real blood.

I pushed Jasmine behind me, angled us so we were not reflected, and grabbed the matches the Master kept by her bedside for her candles. Shaking, I tried to strike one, knowing that a mistake would see us all dead. Matches and wooden hands do not mix. Then Cyclops looked out at me, saw the matches, and his face filled with rage. He started to crawl back towards the crack in the mirror, to slip back into the room. To come for me, for Jasmine, for my sleeping Master.

I struck the match again, held it aloft. Its image in the silvered surface touched Cyclops first. Aurora swooped down, beating her wings in fear, but they only fanned the flames. It caught the soldiers and the delicate beauties in their fancy gowns. As I dropped the match in the empty wine glass and it sizzled out, they screamed and howled, the flames peeling away their painted faces, licking their bodies to charcoal and ash. Smoke wafted from the crack in the mirror, bringing the smell of death with it. I ran over and pulled the cord to drop the black cloth over the mirror, like a curtain over a window, hoping to smother the flames and stop the fire from spreading out into the room.

Soon, but not soon enough, the screaming stopped. As Jasmine and I huddled together, a soft tap-tapping of footsteps approached. Teo walked slowly in.

"Too close, dear moth, your wing's afire!" she said softly. "Terrible things happen when we try to be more than what we are. You see?"

I shook my head. I didn't see at all. We were more than just playthings, someone's little pets. The Marionette Master was so still, I couldn't quite tell if she was alive or... At that moment, I wasn't sure whether I hated her or myself more. She was the one who gave me life, who gave me a taste of a family with whom I could share this life. But I was the one who had needed to sate greed instead of control it.

Teo put her skeletal hand on my shoulder, the wooden bones clacking softly against my hinged shoulder joint. A reminder of what we actually were, not what we wanted to be. "It happened to my Master too, and the Master before her. Once it begins to burn within us, it consumes us..."

Dawn began to pearl the sky, illuminating my Master's body, no longer flesh but petrified wood. If I had a human heart, that is when it would have broken. All was still and quiet, then Jasmine pricked her ears, limped across to the mirror. She sniffed the corner of the black cloth, then caught the cord between her sharp teeth and pulled.

There, in the mirror, were reflections of me, of Teo, and of Jasmine. But nothing of the Master or my family, only piles of ashes from the fire that had consumed the marionettes. The morning sun caught on the smoke swirling and twisting from the rubble. It looked like a sigh. The different spires merged and grew, feeding on the sun's rays, coalesced into an amorphous shape that was smoothed and moulded by unseen hands.

Of smoke and fresh morning light, the last of the Marionette Master looked out at me. She smiled sadly, the ash lifting and dancing around her, then faded into the ebbing gloom as sunlight pierced the room.

I reached into my apron pocket, drew out the blueberry, basil, and rosemary leaves. I wasn't sure where we would end up, but new dangers need ancient protection. We would need to damp down the desires that flared within us. Sprinkling the leaves over the shadow that the master's wooden body cast, Teo, Jasmine, and I sat, scooping handfuls of it into our mouths. A last meal that tasted of sadness and hope, before an unknown future. A consolation of love and shade for little shadows in a world of light.

heartwood, sapwood, spring

Today, it is my turn.

I walk through the main square of our settlement before dawn, to spend the morning in the library originally curated by our grandmothers. The sun is rising as I carefully turn the vellum pages of these most illegal tomes. In some places the ink is blurred. Other words are slashed through, as though our enemy had tried to bleed the very meaning out of them, to leave the stories as nothing but husks. But those blurred, scarred words tell me that the women to whom those stories belonged were fierce. In these folios are the faded scars of their battle wounds.

The words are etched much deeper than our foes understand. The rustle of these delicate pages whisper to me in the early morning light. *Only with an army of words will we bury them*, they say.

Before this library, this town, there was another time entirely. Then, over a century ago, the almost-apocalypse changed everything. Ours became a world split into factions. It was a time of new beginnings and a reversion to simpler ways, but also a time for new enmities. Our enemy sought to erase our past, our identities. Us.

The book I hold in my hands now was my mother's. She died in battle when I was three weeks old. The ink here is not blurred; rather, it is precise, sharp-edged, black as pitch. Her story is my weapon. It kindles the nascent coals of rage in the pit of my belly. The fire roars through my veins.

My mother's skin had been inked during the months before the battle that killed her. Hardly enough time for the words to live within her, which is exactly what the enemy desires. They know the power of the written word. That is why they despise and fear it. They will not touch anything with our words upon it, for they think them cursed.

That is why they do not dispose of our fallen tattooed warriors, but leave them where they lay. In the dark of night and the gray dawn, we creep out to collect them. By lightfall, the remains have disappeared, and it suits the lies they feed their people. *Those women are cursed and rise from the dead, spreading filth and decay in death as in life.* But not all the people believe, and the rebellion is growing, inside the city, Unvard, and outside it.

If the soldiers knew what we did with the bodies, they would burn them where they lay.

Sunlight shafts through the library window, but there is no warmth in its rays. I hold up a sheet of my mother's book to the light, trace my fingertip over the softness that was once her skin before it became page, sewn and bound with ebony hair. Black words against sepia-vellum, fine lines that tell their own story of a young death. Outside, the early morning mist shifts and the light brightens, limning the tattooed words.

history drags me to the open lands,
leaves me naked and newborn,
a woman aflame…

The sky is pale as the moon and it reminds me of my grandmother's witch-silver hair. *My darling Luka*, she always says, *the last of my line.* This morning, she will be preparing the ink, sterilizing her needles and waiting for me.

The rebellion is growing. Next month, I go to battle.

So, today, it is my turn.

* * *

Upper back, cursive

Last of all, they came for our words.

Four generations ago all our books were banned, burned on pyres in flames so fierce, they licked the night sky clean of stars. Our great-grandmothers, young women then, collected the ashes in tiny wooden boxes. The soldiers laughed and kicked them as they left.

Write upon pain of death has remained law since that time.

Stories and history, poetry and science became whispers in the night. The language of the poor, in a world of words uncaught.

The underprivileged and the hunted left Unvard for the borderlands. Our great-grandmothers took those little boxes with them to settlements that were strung out like lighthouses across dangerous shores. To show themselves as friend and forge alliances, the great-grandmothers tattooed poems on their thighs, with ink made with the ashes of the great fires. Those poems were the first language of the dispossessed.

The pen and page were no longer part of the people's armory. So ink and women's flesh became shield and sword.

* * *

Belly, illuminated script (black with red, blue, and gold)
IN PRINCIPIO ERAT VERBUM
(In the beginning was the Word)

* * *

Left thigh, tattooist freehand
Grandmother and I sat in the near-empty rock pools at low tide, starfish scattered at our feet, salt mist wreathing our bare arms. The sea was far from the city – here, we felt safe. Even at five years old, I knew our resistance was secret, as were our sacred texts. They reminded me of the words on Grandmother's skin, which I loved even before I could read.

The waves' foam fizzed over seaweed shallows as Grandmother passed me a lump of charcoal, then closed her hand over mine, guiding it toward the rock wall. Novitiate to her virtuoso, I was initiated into the almost-lost art of writing with cinder and sun-warmed rocks.

We covered the walls with the alphabet, my name, and the names of my foremothers. Then, as the sun set and the sea washed in and stole my written words away, she told me histories, tales tall and true, poetry. She spoke of a future that did not need secrets.

"There is power in words, Luka. More than weapons. We write the words upon us and together we are not just an army. The dead, whose books we tend, and the living? Together, we are the greatest library in the world."

* * *

Left inner forearm, elbow to wrist, old Garamond (framed with green vines)

Heartwood: a tree's incredibly strong support pillar, hollow needles bound together; a word's core from which its meaning is derived.

Sapwood: carries water to the tree's leaves, new wood that turns to heartwood as newer rings are laid down; words as spoken and written, sustaining and transforming language.

Spring: season of renewal that produces tree's growth hormones; to come into being; language passed between writer and reader, speaker and listener.

The enemy seeks to ringbark our stories, to let them wither and die. To winter our words into nothingness.

Never forget that

We are Spring.

* * *

Back right hand and snaking around wrist, cursive

remember the days you wore me

like a shroud,

a wing-caul,

a wrap of forest song. weave me

in the words you sing

your words sit in your chest, like a stone

I wait for them to gather, in a sonnet, a dirge,

a lovesong

you gather them in your cheeks, save

the words for winter

When you speak in morning's frost, weave me

in the words you sing

* * *

Chest, Victorian Gothic (framed with feathered wings)
  Daughter, lover, bereaved
  Story-keeper
  Poet

* * *

Nightfall. The first wave will attack Unvard at three am. My tattoos are still healing, and I settling into them. What are we, if not the accumulated stories of our past and that of our foremothers? I will carry them with me into battle. And if I die, they will interleave my unmarked skin with the inked, to show a life incomplete.

There are seventeen women in my troop and we ready ourselves together by gaslight, low and yellow, smiling at one another as we shave off our tresses. Our hair falls to the floor in waves of copper, mouse-brown, gold, and black. I run my hand over my stubbled scalp and laughter bubbles in my throat. Its unfamiliarity makes me feel free and fierce. The troops we will face tomorrow do not like women who look like us. *That scares them more than our words*, Grandmother used to say.

Around me are the women with whom I will go to battle, stories inscribed on their flesh both scarred and milk-smooth, and I cannot imagine anything more beautiful. Elsewhere in the settlement, the men are preparing too, in their own rituals, their bodies covered with images of dragons and phoenix and gods of old instead of words.

We had not planned to attack for another two weeks, on the new moon. Three days ago, though, we received word that *they* would attack *us* in three days' time, so we must strike tonight. We lace our boots, sheathe swords, and test the sharpness of hand axes against the soft pad of the thumb. Our weavers gather the hair like sheaves of wheat, sifting it by color and plaiting it into ropes they will wash and hang from the windows at dawn. For those who don't return, the hair will be used to bind books of their skin and they will take their place on the library shelves.

The room is quiet, but for the final ritual: we murmur poetry into the night, fragments that will never be written down. It reminds us that some things are ephemeral. If the written word is a tree digging its roots into the alluvium, the spoken word is the last autumn leaves on the rushing breath of winter.

> *one day he would come to reclaim her*
> *on a ship built*
> *from the bones of drowned sailors*

> *night cat, to the night star bound*
> *Three times the merry land, around*
> *Seeks the song, once made her sing*
> *or faded owl, with faded wing*

> *but long*
> *forgot the tendril flames*
> *licking at this skin, a web witch,*
> *burned by men*
> *caught*
> *falling*
> *into my eyes*
> *Myopic, my Narcissus*
> *Leaves me blind*

The words unwind from our mouths, then from one another, to lace together again in new shapes; one moment nonsensical, the next plump with meaning. Finally, I open the door. We fall silent and then the words are gone.

* * *

Unvard's leaders don't think enough of the resistance to black out or even dim its gas lights, and the glow in the sky is a beacon leading us through the forest that drips verdant and lush around us. They know we only have swords and blades to their more sophisticated weapons and think that that makes us weak.

We have walked for hours in silence before we come to the edge of the forest, sharply cut away by the plain of no man's land stretching out between us and the city. The easy part is over and we stay in the shadows, watching. Unvard's ramparts are topped with wicked iron spikes and the towers are well guarded. There is seemingly no way over or through.

Stealth is our advantage here.

The tall grasses ripple, then a series of short whistles signal that the advance party have disarmed the traps that awaited us – the pits full of sharpened sticks, the trip-wire explosives. Our stock of explosives is small, precious, and that will go with the three scouts who are taking the tunnels into enemy territory.

The regiment splits into three – the scouts disappear behind the moss-covered boulders, down a rocky path and out of sight. We wait twenty minutes, twenty-five, enough for them to make their way through the tunnels. It is a small eternity. I breathe slowly to calm my racing heart, fight the need to roll the tension from my shoulders. The first wave moves forward, creeping across no man's land, as light as dancers. The weather has been kind, clouds covering the sky and hiding the fullness of the moon.

We watch from the forest edge, holding our breath.

The moon breaks through the cloud, shining on the warriors out in the open. I wish I could wrap the shadows around us all as I wait for the sentries to spot them. Silently, they crouch or lay flat, unmoving. From our vantage point, the tattooed arms and scalps are like scattered remnants of a living page. Shot through with dark letters, interspersed with the images with which the men are marked.

As the clouds slide across the moon again, dropping the world back into darkness, a gunshot splits the night. We duck behind the cover of the trees and I risk peeking out. The grass is roiling as the first wave run forward. Another crack, then an enormous explosion rends the night, flames so bright I shield my eyes. The subsequent smaller explosions tell me our scouts have hit their target and destroyed the city's armory. Their stockpile of weapons is gone.

I throw my head back and howl our war cry. In the aftermath of the explosion, their arsenal burns and the second wave rushes after the first to the wall, where hidden doors have opened and their army rush towards us. Overhead, bullets pierce the night. Three, five, more of us than I can count fall, but still we run forward, forward, blades raised high over our heads.

Their soldiers wield their swords not just to kill but to carve through the words on our skin and destroy us twice-over.

I slash, and stab, and thunk my axe into flesh and bone. And still I run, screaming and roaring with the rest, covered in blood and gore. I pause. The popping overhead has stopped: their ammunition has run dry. We attack, and run and call, and fight, and will this never end, this mess of cadavers, this whirl of blades?

An explosion throws me backward. The world is ringing, ringing, and the fight, for a moment, is frozen. A click or so to the north, the wall is in ruins and suddenly the city is an open wound. We are on our feet again and now we pour towards *them*. The words of the poetry we spoke to one another in the gaslight rearrange themselves into new shapes, renewing my purpose and moving me forward.

tendril flames licking
at the bones of blind men

Their ranks are in disarray. Our archers light arrows from the fire in the aftermath of the blast. Burning sentries fall from the top of the wall, like embers from a pile of burning books.

Three times the merry land around
Myopic, to the night star bound

And now they are running, a horde of rats back into their holes. We flank them, pushing them backward to the city where they learned to fight, but not to know their adversaries. To the leaders who outlawed knowledge and reduced the people's world to an oubliette.

drowned, faded eyes seek my skin
this the song, once made her sing

One of the soldiers, a young man around my age, is slower than the others and clumsy. He stumbles and falls, sprawling in the grass and mud. I stop, cradling my axe as I stand over him. I will not kill him from behind, like a coward. He begins to crawl forward, then rises slowly and turns to me, arms raised. He looks at my chest, my arms and my hands, covered in my words. His face shows his revulsion, but there is something else. Curiosity, perhaps?

"Are you so blind that you don't see what it is that you fight against? That what you fight *for* is your own servitude?" I say.

He opens his mouth to speak, but nothing comes out.

"Go!" I take a step toward him and he turns, runs after the others.

* * *

The sun will rise soon, so we haven't much time. Mothers and sisters, fathers and cousins have come to take away the dead. They work quickly and quietly, disappearing into the forest with the bodies of seven of my troop among the others. Those of us remaining walk to the gaping, smoldering hole in the wall and whistle softly. Through the ash and dust and the gray pre-dawn, one of the scouts who crept through the tunnels walks towards us. A small crowd follows in her wake – families, lone children, a young couple – and we help them over the ruins, our warriors escorting them across no man's land to trek back to our settlement. The last to come are our remaining two scouts, following three of their soldiers, who wear white scarves around their necks. I tense, but two of them smile and show me the underside of their arms. The word *Free* is inked there in crude lettering.

I turn to the third and it is the young man I chased from the battlefield. He is cuffed, but calm. "I am ready to learn," is all he says.

I nod to him and smile, hoping that he really is ready for the road that lies ahead. It is one of uncertainty and exile and *knowing*; that is never easy. But in knowledge is freedom. This is a road I have walked all my life, and my book, inscribed and life-scarred, will one day join the others in our library.

But not today. I am not yet fully written.

One day, there will be more of *us* than *them*. Our stories have a thousand different beginnings and endings. They cannot be buried or forgotten forever. We have spent four generations recreating, remaking the stories on our own bodies from the relics of old words. Our poetry, the language of the soul that lies inside us like fossils, waiting to be uncovered, will continue to shape us in ways unexpected and true.

Whether charcoaled words on sea cave walls
Or books of tattooed skin,
The voices of spring braided with sapwood
And autumn words breezing to uncharted shores.

her night of savagery sung

Three AM. The witching hour. The time that sleep is closest to death, when the membrane between worlds is thin and malleable. At three am, all manner of creatures will find a way to slink through the veil.

Over the lawn fronting an ordinary house a claw, demon-steel sharp, rends the air, opening a wound in the caul of night. Amanita, queen of the lightshifters, draws her hand back, and then slithers through from the other side. The air around her crackles as the silver fissures she has stepped through seal over. She crosses the damp grass, to the lonely bedroom window facing the street. Delicately grasping the sill, she peers through it.

The bedroom is dark, the weak moonlight and harsher streetlight spilling through the curtain-cracks casting grim shadows. The young man, Adam, is asleep in the bed, chest rising and falling with each breath. She could not possibly recall the names of all her prey, but Adam is particularly memorable. That is why she returns, over and over. Amanita flicks her tongue in and out, tasting the night. The witching hour is sweet as ambrosia. She breathes in, sucking the last of the illumination from the room. The green numbers on the digital clock flicker before it, too, goes black.

Like the mushroom from which she took her name, Amanita inhabits the netherworld between the living and the dead. At times she is woman-shaped, others she is a heavy stone, full of crags and covered in eldritch moss, resting on the chests of dreamers and paralysing them in their sleep. Mostly, she stretches out like a web across the worlds, awaiting the lightning strike of fear to call her. Sharp as ozone, she blooms under its touch, breaking through into this world and seeking out those places where dread coagulates like mud after the rain. Scales of ice cover her skin, shining with the light stolen from the bedrooms of a thousand dreamers. Still, it is not enough to have given her permanent, solid form. She could be blown away by the merest hint of breeze. Although, she thinks, it would need to be more than an ordinary breeze from the mortal world. Perhaps the winds of Ezahir could break her apart and scatter her to the seven worlds. Just like they did her sister Verna, who developed a taste for things unnatural to a lightshifter. Lust. Soft flesh. The headiness of human marrow.

It hadn't ended well for anyone.

In the room, cotton sheets rustle as Adam kicks, turns, settles. *Does he know that* he *awakened* me? *A thunderstorm stirring the fungus spores in the roots of a birch tree. A flash in the darkness, a call that is a burn.*

Amanita's flesh dulls to grey and her body ripples, until she is a wisp of smoke drifting through the tiny space between window and wooden frame. Her incorporeal senses pierce the thick shadows. The room smells of soap and sweat. Her tongue again flicks in and out. The taste of the air tells her his dreaming is not far away. Adam's eyes move rapidly back and forth beneath their lids. His fears are gathering themselves, crawling to the surface, slinking through his mind. Amanita is *greedy* for them, wants to reach out and pluck them from him.

That will ruin the taste, she cautions herself.

Her breath turns the air frigid, an otherworld cold of the in-between lands. In the suddenly freezing air, Adam's breath plumes; his bare legs, tangled in the sheets, are pinpricked with goose bumps. Lying on his back, arms outspread, he appears crucified.

The lightshifter, nebulous as mist, hovers over his body. She reaches through his skin, runs her hands along his clavicle, his rib cage. His heart beats faster and he groans in his sleep. The other hand she places oh-so-lightly on his temple. Slipping just two fingers under the skin, she feels his pulse, fluttering like a baby bird thrown from the nest. Terror runs right through him. It *owns* him.

It is just as she remembered. But there is something else too…a shallowness of breath…something else unfamiliar. She is too hungry to stop to investigate further, and weaves her way down to sit at his side, removing her hands from him. Kneeling at the side of Adam's bed, Amanita licks the tips of her fingers, tastes the delicious secrets he hides.

Secrets borne of cowardice and rancour. They look for her edges, try to stitch themselves within her the way they do with fragile humans. Instead, they find something entirely different; the dormant spores of a lightshifter, waiting to be shaped. Her skeleton and the excavated terrors knit themselves together in a new form. They sting and bubble under her still-forming skin. Becoming whole again, shaped by Adam's disquietude, is agonising. But for a lightshifter, pain is pleasure; it makes her smile. She runs her tongue over her new, sharp teeth. The young man whimpers in his sleep, pulls his legs back under the covers.

Amanita stands, stretches, and climbs onto the bed, a bruise of malice in a tenebrous body. Under her skin, his phobias and doubts, his most awful thoughts, seethe. She crouches on his chest, a heavy weight of dread made into flesh. He moans again, her weight pinning him to the mattress. Leaning forward, she kisses his lips, lightly as can be. Then she opens her mouth, covering his lips and nose, smothering his cries. Silently, she screams his fears back into him, feeling them rush through him, like bad blood.

Her eyes close as the nightmare begins to crush him.

Careful, she tells herself. Too much and her poison will be fatal. Pulling her face back from his, her body mirrors the adrenaline response it provokes in him, the primal echo of his need to flee.

With a jolt he opens his eyes, and with the last of her breath she breathes out the moon-and-streetlight so he can see her in its wan glow. Waits for his eyes to widen as he realises that he cannot move, seeing her sitting on his chest in hag form. This is how it has been countless times before; nightmares are consistent this way.

Instead, he grabs Amanita's throat. *This* is what she detected earlier, though she is not prepared for it. The pain is superbly terrible; she bares her teeth and digs her talons into his shoulders, drawing blood. It sings as it meets the scales on her skin, a sound that rings across all seven worlds as the chime of a sunken bell, the last note of a bone-cello concerto, the first song of the sirens. The winds of Ezahir begin to stir.

The shock loosens Adam's grip just for a moment; Amanita loosens her form, becomes smoke and fog once again, glimmering with points of light like dying stars. Although he does not know it, *this* is what she has been waiting for – the very reason she has visited Adam since he was a child. She wraps herself around him like a shroud. His body slackens, but it is not his body she is interested in. No, it is the *soul* that calls to lightshifters, although that is far too crude a term to describe the delicate ephemera that composes human beings.

Amanita holds Adam's soul tightly in her arms. She begins to pull, and stretch, and unmake him, as the winds blow in from the forgotten corners of Ezahir and all the barren places in between. Stretches herself and Adam like a net, across the borders, wider and further, drinking in his agony. The winds squall, and gust, and blow through them, drawing borders on their impossibly elongated forms. Making depthless black lakes from his fears and star-filled skies from her pleasure.

The winds break them into seven pieces – one for each of the worlds – and Amanita digs each piece of herself into his, a radicle searching through loam. *I did not make the same mistake as you, sweet Verna,* she thinks, remembering her sister, whose banishment to the seven worlds was punishment instead of power. Amanita moves through the broken parts of Adam, swirls herself through him like ink in water. His last memories are not the fears that she has become so familiar with, but of the bitter oranges preserved in honey that he ate as a child, and the smell of the sea mist before a storm. Then he is gone, a river tinged forever with indigo ink, the two inseparable from one another.

Amanita settles over the seven worlds, pushing into their soil and their seas. Settling under their skies and scattering her goddess spores, no longer awaiting the call of dread to shape her. Now *she* will shape and mould and make all of her choosing. Skin-hungry, she salts the seven worlds with her desire, and they answer with a song like the cries of a dreaming man, screaming to be woken.

song of opal, song of stone

"I will go to the weeping women, then." Nico stared at Father as he bound her wounded arm too tightly. He glared at her, a look she knew he would not have dared had once-betrothed Kherys been by her side. But Kherys was lost to her, had left her with only the injury to her arm as a reminder of him.

"You won't survive that shore, daughter." Father marched her outside their hut on the cliffs, forced her to look down at the beach where the weeping women stood, bones calcified, like rocks eroded over endless years. Most had sunk to their knees, unable to bear the weight of their grief, hands clasped to their breast or outstretched towards the horizon. The women faced the sea, the spray salting their skin, breeze tugging at their bodies. But it couldn't fell them, for they had long since grown firm roots into the sand, were turned to rock and scarfskin, faces frozen in exquisite agony.

"See them there, Nico? And what do you think they can do for you now?"

Her throat was dry. "I'm not one of the wild children, it's true, but there must be more to the world than that mob... The women, they know. They always knew."

Father shook his head, picked up the pack he had left by the door. Slinging it over his shoulder, he turned and walked away from Nico towards the grasslands and the dust plains beyond, where the air would dry even the most stubborn sobbing. Nico held herself steady against the urge to chase after him, to beg him to take her too. For it was Kherys, betrothed to Nico, who had carried all of father's hopes. Kherys, who wore grasses plaited about his throat and siren song in his hair, and had broken father by leaving Nico. Father didn't care that something had curled tight and died inside Nico too.

She waited for the distance to swallow her father. He didn't look back at her, not even as he shouted his last words.

"Go to the shore then, to the weeping women. Drown yourself at their feet, for all I care. I can no longer bear the sight of you."

* * *

The weeping women were lined by the hundreds on the white sand shore, cliffs inked in shadows behind them. The mourning cries of the grey gulls wheeled through the air and the sand was soft under Nico's feet as she walked towards them. Their chests rose and fell very slowly as they breathed. An eternal stream of sluggish tears ran down their faces.

Near the waterline lay one who had died, her remains left as a hollow shell for the tide to wash away. Nico remembered the stories all the children learned about the women. About the stonemothers who had left them to their fate.

They don't die for many years, but when they do the children cut their bodies open to mine the opals that hide inside them, all fire and reflected ocean.

Nico leaned close to the carapace, gently touched the crumbling remains flecked with opal chips. Her chest felt heavy as she brushed the chips with her fingertips. They were the women's unwept tears, lying like fossils inside them. If only she had her own tears to spill, to show the loneliness stretched sky-wide inside her.

She wished that once-betrothed Kherys was with her, but there was no return from where he had gone. Had he really abandoned her too? Once he would have marvelled at the opal tears; she shivered at the thought of what he may do with those fragile jewels now.

The older men used to cry too, shifting the sands with their moans. But they were easily tempted and turned from their despair. It was nothing, then, for the sirens to call them far out to sea.

Their bones washed up not long after, the tide clattering them against the women's legs. That was the only day that their eyes were dry.

The women were not so easily turned, although one, now and again, would tear herself from the earth and drag herself into the waves. She would turn to foam, laced across the shore. Her eyes became shell, her body the tiny worms that burrow in the shallows.

It is the tears of the weeping women that embittered the water, turning it to brine.

They shed their skins on nights of the king tides and the gangs of wild children sometimes found their scales washed onto the beach, stringing them with the opals in strange mandalas that they hung from the leaning trees on the cliff top. On bright nights the mandalas sang and cried out, a lighthouse song to scare away the bravest of sailors who might have tried their luck on these shores.

What is their lament?

The tears flowed faster, carving trails into the women's sandstone skin. The waves lapped at Nico's feet, salt and shed skin breaking over her. It called to her, not as siren song or mandala warning, but as knowledge. They wept because of the children. Nico touched her own dry cheeks, skin that had never known the salt of sadness. It was the children, with no tears of their own and who never cared much for the women's grief. The children, who could not cry but pressed the precious stones they carved from the dead into their own sun-hardened flesh. Branding themselves forever and rendering them impervious to the harm of human hands. They would sneak, snaky, to hunt along the shore, with not a thought for the women they had left behind. For the ones they had cut open. Their blades rusted with the dead ones' briny blood; the opals adorning them spread like calluses as the children aged, as the years fixed to them like oysters on the rocks. When green-black storms blew in from the horizon, the children keened the mandalas' song. It was not a sound meant to be made by human tongues.

There was nothing to tie Nico to this place anymore. Her betrothal to Kherys had been her hope for a new way, beyond the wild mob. What was her way forward now? Would the stonemothers answer Nico if she gave them what they cried for? They stared silently towards the waves as Nico unwound the bandage from her arm. As she walked among them, blood ran from her wound to mark the sand, a breadcrumb trail to lead lost children back home.

* * *

Nico hid in the scrub and sand dunes, waiting until the ocean was calm and the scrimshaw moon trailed its light over the water. She waited. She remembered, pressing the sea-grass poultice firmly onto her wound to disguise its telltale scent.

See the women weeping: they abandoned their children for the shore. Now their children hunt in packs and have taken the shores for their own.

Hunt and worse. Nico had seen Kherys spearing the old men in the next village, then dragging the bodies off to the sea caves. He howled through the streets of that ghost town, laughing as he spied Nico staring down from the clock tower. He beckoned to her and when she drew close, he bit her arm savagely. "You've no rights here. You're not one of us." He licked her blood from his chin.

"Remember me, Nico. *Fear me.* Next time, I'll drag you off to join the old ones myself..." He hissed and growled gutturally, the language of the wild children.

Kherys' words had the sting of truth. She was not one of the mob, nor an eternally grieving stonemother, nor a father set out alone across the plains without thought for his daughter. Not Nico-betrothed, not daughter Nico anymore. Just a girl waiting on the shore, looking to carve the future from uncertainty.

Lightning flashed far out to sea as the children slithered out of their caves and crept across the sand. Nico froze, willing them away from her and hoping that was enough. They stopped, cocked their heads and sniffed, grunting as the scent of the bloodied sand reached them. The women stood as a stone forest. There were only a dozen or so among the hundreds whose chests did not rise and fall. The children would not normally risk going deep into that forest only for the still ones' opals – they preferred the lone dead – but the blood trail promised hunting too. Some of the children crawled with noses close to the ground, seeking its source. The stench of drying seaweed and eels rotting in the sun flooded the night as the other children cut into the bodies of the still women. Cutting, grasping, pulling; the flesh crumbled like old coral as they dug through the remains then tossed their treasure onto the ground behind them.

The remaining weeping women were still, forever staring out to the world's edge. Faces streaked in dirt and the women's grim remains, the children stood as they finished, sheathing their blades. Without warning the women struck, a blur of stony arms and whirlwinds of sand from which Nico shielded her eyes.

She opened them as the night became still again. In the distance, ship sails flapped. On the cliffs above, the mandalas were silent. There was no need to skulk across the sand, for the women had wrapped every last child in an unforgiving embrace, tight against their chests. Blood stained the women as the children struggled ferociously, but did not make a sound. Hands of scale and rock covered their mouths and, after long moments in which the sea shushed over the shore and the sand turned cold under Nico's feet, the children stopped moving. Where the tears fell upon them, their flesh ossified, pale and delicate as a coral fan or the bleached driftwood littering the dunes.

Kherys was not among them. It left her uneasy.

Opals were scattered carelessly across the sand, their colours sparking against it. Nico picked them up, one by one, until she could hold no more. They were warm to the touch.

Sitting on the sand, she collected the gems in her lap, moonlight darting fish-quick through their shallows. The first she pressed into her cheek, soft and yielding, and it whispered of the ceaseless rhythms of time. Then another into her shoulder, more still in a line down her arm, then her tender calves and feet.

Sheathed in the dreams and sorrows of the stonemothers, Nico stood and walked towards the water as the soldier crabs picked gently at the rubble left behind.

Her feet left shadows of footprints in the sand. The water was colder than she remembered and she drew back. She had come to the weeping shore for answers and had given the wild children back to the women.

The opals pulsed in her flesh. Here were not just endings; here was past and future and glorious uncertainty, they said. Nico stood. Out there in the dark starry ocean was *onward*. Only onward, with stones studding her flesh and the brackish embrace of the sea.

Beyond the last line of breakers is the gate at the edge of the world. A new voice, soft and flaring opal fire, echoed through her. The voice of the mothers, answering Nico at last.

She ran forward and dived under the waves. Though her legs grew tired and her arms sore, she swam along the moon's trail, following the sound of storms raging beyond the gate. As she swam, hands soft as sea grass pulled at her feet. From behind her, lamiae mouths promised the knowledge of the universe if she would just join them undersea, where they would weave starfish into her hair and coral around her human heart.

The hands stroked Nico's ankles and she slowed, partly treading water. Were they sirens, or echoes of the past and future, or shadows of the women, calling and cajoling? A strong, calloused hand closed around the top of her arm, pulling her backward. Thrashing about, Nico turned. Kherys smiled, showing his sharp, yellow teeth, pulling her towards him.

She had lost enough to him already. Taking a deep breath, she ducked underwater, wrapping her free hand around Kherys' wrist and taking him with her. Lamiae hands grabbed at her throat, dragged her down through the darkness. She folded her legs around Kherys' waist as he struggled and kicked out. The hands brushed the opals and drew back as though burned. A harpy voice screeched through the depths.

Suspended between the ocean surface and its floor, bubbles of oxygen and light, both, streamed from her skin. In their glow, the ghosts of the weeping women who had dragged themselves from the shore reached out towards Nico and Kherys. Their faces were animated, expressive. Hungry.

Pale limbs ripped Kherys away from Nico. Wormlike fingers burrowed into his flesh as the light faded. Face contorted in terror, he reached uselessly for Nico as he disappeared into the inky depths.

Nico surfaced, spluttering, horrified, triumphant. The dark, dead space that Kherys and Father had left behind her sank after Kherys, cast off just as they had discarded her. *See?* she imagined saying to them. *I can be fierce too.* Behind her, the waves rolled into the shore.

Lightning flashed through the grey clouds and it was there, just ahead; an enormous gate of curlicued iron and copper, rust and ancient verdigris. It shifted as Nico swam a little to the right, then it disappeared. Back to the left and it shimmered into sight again. She struck out towards it, scared that it may be a mirage and that the ghostly creatures beneath song of opal, song of stone

the sea may have her after all. But the gate was sturdy under her hands. She grasped it as best she could and leaned her head against it, breathing heavily.

Beyond the gate at the edge of the world, the sky was stormy green, then a sunset gold, then visceral red, swirling and ebbing towards stranger shores. From her right, a black ship with tattered sails and a faded figurehead swept towards Nico, heading for the gate. Tenebrous against the tides, the ship made Nico shudder. Her flesh pinched around the stones. The pain calmed her.

A ladder dropped down the side of the ship and Nico climbed up to the deck. It was unmanned, a shadowy skeleton of a ship rather than a substantial vessel. Standing on the deck, the words of the stonemothers coursed through her. *This is a dead world, Nico, of weeping women and absent men and desolate children. These are impossible lands, impossible seas. Here is the gate at the edge of the world. Here are the songs that will see you through...*

One by one she plucked the opals from her skin and tossed them into the air. As each landed, the ship emerged from the shadows and into existence: a redwood deck, cerulean sails, a mast studded with copper mermaids. As Nico's wounds bled, they sang in the voices of those who were silenced so long ago. The ship flashed with opal lustre and the mandalas on the cliff cried out a new song, singing out the end of this time and the beginning of the next.

And when you have seen the women weep and your men go back to their beginnings; when the wild children are no more, only then will your time begin anew.

The gate gusted open and Nico took the ship's wheel.

a wide sky multiplied

Before time began. An island of exiled gods at the edge of the world.

Here, earth is stars unwound.

The god Basari has been here forever and a little more. His crime? Unable to bear the idea of death, he tricked the Queen of the Underworld into a boat that sailed for the end of the universe. The Queen found her way back of course; she always does. And she returned with a demand for retribution on her tongue.

"Send him to a place where life does not exist," she said, then paused, wondering if that was enough. The Council of Gods held its breath as galaxies spored and collapsed, spored again.

"Better still: send him to a place where life is uncertain."

So Basari was banished to a world where he presses the bones of the dead into rock and clay and sand. He breathes softly on the remains of fallen creatures, covers them in peat and layers of time, unsure whether he wants them to be hidden forever or one day found and live again. He does these things without thinking, letting his hands move through the earth and her elements, as though humming a harmony over a bass resonance, unwittingly writing a melancholic tune.

One day, the sun shines a little brighter, the ocean is kinder with her tides, and Basari's voice finds a different refrain. He doesn't mean to sing to life a girl from clay and the ribs of giants. Doesn't mean to take ten millennia of existence and sculpt it into something small and kind and curious. How can he know that he is shaping sadness and searching into flesh and bone? But as his song dies away, there she is.

"Mary," he calls her, and she answers with a smile. He knows that the more complicated the creation, the simpler the name should be. There are rules around such things that should not be broken. The right name,

Basari knows, can contain a creature in its form, within the boundaries to which they are born.

Sometimes the rules are wrong.

At first, Mary is content to walk with her father as he tells her stories of forgotten peoples, galaxies he created and burned, worlds that he will make for her. They speak of smaller things too – the indigo flowers that open their faces to the sun each morning, the soil of the deadlands that smells of burnt sugarcane at sunset.

Mary is the only constant against Basari's uncertainty. He clings to her, tries to keep her by his side, but the Council of Gods has done its work well. This is not a place where anyone, least of all the daughter of a god, can settle. Too soon, Basari's stories are no longer enough.

Mary hears the fungi chanting, far away, and asks her father, "What are those sounds?"

He answers the only way he knows how. Basari sings for his daughter, shimmering tales of love and loss, horror and brightness in all his notes and the spaces in between. It never quite dies, but weaves itself around her, trying to make Basari Mary's only home. To make her forget the call of places where earth is stars unwound.

Basari cannot see that she is simultaneously too big and too small for that. As he sleeps, in the wake of the only lullaby his voice will ever know, the mountains and the forest call to Mary. In answer to her father's song, they cantillate *life, life, life* across the deadlands, where the fossils of expired gods lie like dying stars, collapsing under the weight of forgetting.

She smiles, laughs a little as she walks towards them; towards the place that begins to unwind into something *other*. Something *more*. Where the air is different, crackling with promise.

The rain drizzles through the canopy as she wanders the wildwood that covers the foothills. Beneath her feet, the fungi deep in the earth hums. Its voice is like the beating of an infant's heart. For a moment, she is back in the beginning, being shaped under Basari's hands and voice, her bones shining with the cobalt light of new life through eggshell-fine skin.

Mary stops in a clearing, feels the rain on her skin and opens her mouth to catch drops on her tongue. She spins once, twice, an almost-dance, and sniffs the air. The smell of rich loam and the ocean-salt tang of rubus flowers tickle her nose. Yet there is something unsettling. She stands very still, waiting. The beating below the ground quickens and the fungi around her climb the trees, dying off on the forest floor and sporing on the damp bark. As though running from something.

She tenses, her body coiled tight as winter bracken.

A flash of lightning opens the sky, a creator wrapping her arms around the universe. Then another, an arc of wild energy earthing at her feet. Bright, hot pain courses through her and everything goes black.

* * *

1799. Dorset. United Kingdom.

A crack of lightning through the dreary sky and the first fat raindrops. The three women in heavy crinoline skirts, watching the polo match, take shelter under an old elm tree. The youngest holds a toddler in her arms. The child, Mary, blinks placidly as the thunder groans and the storm gathers.

The sky splits again, an arc of electricity striking the highest point: the elm tree. It crackles through the wood, lighting up the trunk from within and setting the leaves aflame. The women do not even have the chance to scream as it blasts them off their feet.

As they lie broken and smouldering, the horsemen shout and dismount, running toward them. They gather the baby from the damp ground onto which she has been flung. She has no pulse. One bolts for the doctor, another cradles her gently, places his fingers at her tiny wrist, her fragile throat. Wait! A flutter – irregular, yes, but *there*. Steadier now, steady, then the child gasps and opens her eyes.

The lightning has brought something extraordinary with it, across time and space, and fixed it into a different shape. The accidental daughter of a forgotten god who, a few moments and millions of years before, had stood in a forest on the edge of the world, is now a babe in arms. Mary remembers none of that, the time *before* curled, fossilised, inside her. Unknowing, she stares out upon the strange world into which the lightning had brought her, reborn.

* * *

"You're too rambunctious for a young lady!" Mother says for the umpteenth time, but she smiles all the same, waves to eight-year-old Mary who dashes along the shoreline, sure-footed despite the slippery shale and loose rocks tumbling into the sea. If she could run to the horizon and beyond, she would, to escape everything: her ridiculous skirts and frills; the loneliness of *unbelonging* (she knows it isn't a word, but it's the only one that's right for how she feels); her very self. The horizon, however, has a most troubling habit of constantly moving away, no matter how fast she chases it.

She skids to a halt, her brother's frustrated yells as he tries to keep up with her finally fading away. Spying a hidey-hole in the base of the cliffs that hug the beach, Mary scrambles up toward it. It is a shallow cave, just big enough for her to sit in, her head almost touching the roof. She feels like a lost explorer, like those in her brother's books that she reads secretly in the lavender patch behind their house, until he starts calling her again. Wanting to hide for as long as possible, she lies on her back, pulling her feet up and trying to make herself as small as possible.

Staring up at the ceiling she blinks once, twice, sure that her eyes must be playing tricks on her. Instead of smooth rock, there are indentations: whorled snail shells, delicate fish skeletons, feathers and peculiar, stick-limbed creatures that are *almost* familiar. Calmness settles inside her, like nothing she has ever felt before. *They are like me,* she thinks. Here, yet not here. Like something waiting to be born; for real life to begin.

She reaches out, tracing them with her fingertips. Her touch leaves a trail of faint blue light, like a nebula of dying stars. As she pulls her hand away, it sheds three fingernails: pinky, ring, middle. It does not hurt, or bleed. It is as though she simply does not need them anymore. A roar, primal and uncontrolled, curls from the pit of her belly and she feels as though she might burst out of her very skin.

The roar turns into a yelp as her brother grabs her ankle and pulls her out of the cave that, for a moment, felt like home.

* * *

The alleged wisdom of the early nineteenth century is not kind.

Fossil hunting is no decent choice for a woman.

But for Mary, now twenty-nine and constantly combing the seashore for its hidden treasures, it is not a choice, but the very thing that she lives for. She could no more stop this than the ocean could decide it would no longer tide. What does it matter anyway, whether people think she is respectable? Her parents are both long passed and her brother has gone to London, from where he sends perhaps a Christmas card or letter, when he thinks of it. There is little to tether her to a world that she does not fit.

Today, dusk has come and gone, and the night is pinned with stars bravely holding back the darkness between worlds. Waves shush upon the shore and, in the moonlight, Mary gently shifts the pieces she has found that day into an endless array of permutations.

Ammonite,

     plesiosaur vertebrae,

          ray-fins

coiled shells mathematically precise,

          invertebrates indeterminate

Although she would not speak of this to anyone, she is looking for an answer in the poetry of fossils. She is looking for a way to explain to herself who she is. These remnants of the past speak a language that she understands. Lock them with one another, they sing of a different soul. Unwind, shift into another combination, and they whisper of worlds beyond the wide sky that concertinas and multiplies itself across time and space.

But today the waves continue to shush and the heavens do not open to reveal any secrets to Mary. All she knows is that she does not fit this body, this form, so tiny and insubstantial. She stands, walks to the water's edge, and howls out to the sea. The only answer is a flutter of memory of dank forests and bones that shine like infinitesimal universes trapped within flesh.

* * *

Years pass and Mary writes secret, ephemeral poetry with shells and bones she finds on the shale shores. Once, she thinks she has found what she is looking for. The next morning, she wakes to find her body has shed her ears, in the way it shed her fingernails so long ago. They lie on her pillow like pale pink seashells. Although it doesn't bother her, she changes her hairstyle to cover that strange absence.

But other than that one time, no matter how hard she tries, the answer is never quite there. Sometimes, she gets close and she *thinks* she remembers things that can't possibly be true. A deep voice telling her that the blood of giants runs through her veins. A long ago lullaby that made the earth tremble beneath her feet. The very first time she awoke, under a pale-gold sky, cradled in impossible arms. A lightning storm that split the world open forever.

Then comes the night of the new storm, fierce enough to uproot trees and send mud and rocks tumbling down cliffs into the sea below. The landslide is loud enough to wake Mary and she sits up, turns on the gas lamp, listening to the tempest shriek and crash, as though the gods themselves are warring from all corners of the earth. She fights the urge to run outside, to let the gale lash at her. To carry her away.

Dozing, she dreams that she is an enormous creature swimming through the depths, floating in briny currents and diving down to the depths, where molten rock bubbles up through the ocean floor. As though, at last, the fossils have formed the ballad that has freed her. Waking just before dawn, as the squall quietens, she is unsurprised to find salt drying on her skin.

She doesn't bother with her coat when she leaves the house, even though the rain mists and spits. It is still dark, but she wants to get to the shore before anyone else, to comb through the earth the landslide has opened up.

The early grey light shows that a great chunk of the cliff has given way. Rubble has piled up on the water's edge and the beach is, for the most part, impassable. She walks toward the site of the slide, heart beating fast. With her gloved hands, she shifts the soil, brushing it away from what lies underneath. Mary works until her fingers are cramped and her knees are bruised from crawling. But, at last, there it is. The skull is long, its elongated bill filled with rows of sharp teeth. The eye sockets the size of both her fists held together. Its spine stretches out behind it, elegant and fine: the ribs are precise and perfect.

Exhausted, exhilarated, Mary removes her gloves and reaches out to gently touch the spindled bones of its flippers. She closes her eyes, imagining – *feeling* – the creature gliding through the depths, darting from the leviathans of the deep, breaching toward the glittering sunlight.

Should she lie down next to it, it would easily be three times her height. The creature's size fits the wanting that waits within her. It is part of a world that is constantly remaking itself, but that does not forget. It tells her, *You are part of something vast and much larger than most can imagine.*

She turns toward the horizon. In the moment before the sun spills over, a cobalt aurora blazes across the sky. Mary calls out and it opens like a fan. From far beyond, her brethren call back. She begins to slough off her human form, running her fingertips from collarbone to belly, cutting through the fabric of her clothes and opening a seam in her skin. Unbuttoning her jacket, she reaches inside, peels the seam back, opens up the body in which she has lived for so long. The arms go limp as she slides along the tendons and muscles fitted to the ulna, the radius, the clavicle, prying apart the rib cage then reaching out from inside. With that one reach outside her human form, it is as though she can breathe properly for the first time. Bending, twisting, she slips out of her skin, discards it like the ill-fitted suit it always was, leaving it lying alongside her last and greatest find.

Uncontained, she is as sharp and pale as moonlight, and shines across the ocean to unwind the stars and breathe life into galaxies curled tight inside the fossils of gods.

publication history

"Of Starfish Tides," *Next* anthology, CSFG (2013).

"A Silver Thread Between Worlds," *F is for Faerie,* edited by Rhonda Parrish, Poise and Pen Press (2019).

"Rag and Bone Heart," *Phantazein* anthology, edited by Tehani Wessely, Fablecroft Publishing (2014).

"The Psychometrist," *Postscripts 32/33: Far Voyager* anthology, PS Publishing (2014).

"Sundark and Winterling," *British Fantasy Society Journal,* issue 13 (2014).

"Husk and Sheaf," *SQ Mag,* Edition 22 (2015).

"The Cartographer's Price," *Mythic Delirium Issue 3.1* (2016).

"A Nightingale's Map of the City," *Metaphorosis Magazine* (February 2017).

"At the Still Point," *Lackington's Magazine,* Issue 14 (Spring 2017).

"Blackhearts and Sorrowsong," *A Miscellany of Death and Folly,* edited by Mark Beech, Egaeus Press (2019).

"A Solace of Shadows," *Three Crows Magazine,* Issue 7 (August 2020).

"Heartwood, Sapwood, Spring," *Sword and Sonnet Anthology*, edited by Aidan Doyle, Rachel K. Jones, and E. Catherine Tobler (2018).

"A Wide Sky Multiplied," *Syntax and Salt*, Volume 2 (2019).

acknowledgments

A big thank you to Scarlett R. Algee, for the amazing opportunity to send these stories out into the world together.

To my writing group, the Arctic Pandas – for the feedback, the kindness and the laughs.

To my soul-sister Angie Rega, and all the tea, lime marmalade and fairy tales both past and future.

To Angela Slatter, whose kindness and friendship are boundless. Without Ange, this collection would not have been possible, and I am grateful beyond words.

To my "Funky Family", and my amazing mum and dad.

A little note to my darling pooch, Bosley. You sat by me while I wrote these words, and brought infinite joy and love to my life. I will miss you forever.

And thanks, as always, to my partner, Griff – for everything and beyond.

about the author

Suzanne is a Melbourne, Australia-based writer, a graduate of Clarion South and an Aurealis Awards finalist. Her short stories have appeared in various anthologies, and in *Mythic Delirium*, *Lackington's* and *The Dark*, among others, while two *Broken Cities* novellas were released by Falstaff Books in 2019 and 2021. Suzanne's tales are inspired by fairytales, ghost stories and all things strange, and she can be found online at suzannejwillis.webs.com